Our
MOTHER
away from
HOME

Adventures of a High School Activities Director

By
Tanya Katnic

Annabooks, LLC.
Rancho Mirage

Our Mother Away from Home
Copyright © 2021, Tanya Katnic. All Rights Reserved

Published in the United States by **Annabooks, LLC.**
69 Bordeaux, Rancho Mirage, CA 92271
www.annabooks.com

Manufactured in the United States of America

10 9 8 7 6 5 4 3 2 1

Library of Congress Cataloging-in-Publication Data is available:

ISBN-13: 978-0-9911887-7-2

Acknowledgements

I am thankful for support, inspiration, and wisdom from Roxanne Brandt, Jane McIntosh Jordan, Noelle Reminiskey, Pamela Gibbons Toomey, Annabooks, my former students, and my family.

Chapter One - September

A thin sliver of sunlight inched its way through Cassie Greenwood's bedroom curtains, casting a light in morning welcome. She squeezed one eye in the brightness, and the other eye landed on the ringing clock. 8:00 a.m. Today is the first day of the school year for the faculty of Bennington High School in Oakview, California, a brief pause before the students descend on the land of the Jets on Thursday. Three days of faculty meetings, arranging classrooms, and putting up bulletin boards. And "sleeping in" until 8:00.

Bennington, called Bennie for short, was established in 1973 around the time when Elton John's "Bennie and the Jets" arrived on the music scene as part of his album *Goodbye Yellow Brick Road*. The mascot was a no-brainer for Bennie's inaugural administration, though it serves as a strange symbol of the school.

Cassie had slept in her favorite T-shirt, which read "Keep calm and call a Vice Principal." As the Director of Activities, she also held the title of Vice Principal. Bennington, a small school of 350 students in grades 9-12, doubled up a few jobs. Cassie's was one of them. She scheduled all student activities, such as the dances and rallies, and oversaw the Associated Student Body program.

An aura of purple royally draped Cassie's bedroom--from lavender to plum--reflecting her love for the color. Along with pillows, stuffed animals, and bedding adorned in purple were trophies and ribbons from her stellar softball career at both Bennington and California State University at Monterey Bay. At CSUMB, Cassie earned a four-year athletic scholarship for softball and graduated Summa cum Laude with a degree in English. She subsequently earned a Master's degree in educational administration at the same college, with a dream of moving up to administration.

This was her childhood bedroom, minus the twin bed in which she slept for many years. When her adoptive parents died five years ago, making her an orphan with no siblings to consult, she decided to move back into their home and graduate to a queen-sized bed.

Cassie's father Herb was a beloved football coach at Westfield Junior College, and her parents died when the small plane in which they were travelling on a recruiting trip crashed into the misty mountains above San Francisco. She could not even fathom selling the Southern California house, where so many memories lay beyond every corner, etched in the walls and pictures and trinkets. Having no rent or mortgage made the move even sweeter.

When she caught her reflection in her bathroom mirror, Cassie's green eyes assessed her profile: five feet four; curly, long brunette hair; skin kissed by the summer sun; physique toned by her three-mile runs.

Our Mother Away from Home

Inwardly, she was a strong young woman, devoted to education and fiercely protective of her friends, who willingly now serve as her substitute family.

Her shoulders erect, Cassie stood ready for another school year, her tenth and last at Bennington.

Starting next year, she would be the Activities Director at Marina Shores High School, a brand-new school of a potential 1,000 students located half an hour south of Oakview. It would be a new beginning for Cassie, a new chapter in her educational journey that she was ready to tackle. What an exciting time!

The school had already chosen a mascot—the dolphin—as the campus overlooked the Pacific Ocean. The school would have marine biology classes in coordination with an aquarium that the city of Marina Shores built within walking distance of the school. The STEAM program (Science.Technology.Engineering.Arts.Mathematics.) was in the creation process, and the school would be top-notch in terms of technology. Buildings, including a state-of-the-art gym, were all under construction.

Cassie was one of the few employees who were hired thus far, as the district started with the administration first. Head coaches would be chosen next. Once numbers of new and transfer students in grades 9-12 trickled in, a base of teachers and staff would be hired.

Marina Shores' principal, Dr. James Castleberry, was a seasoned administrator who had earned the respect of school district officials and of his colleagues over the years. This would be his last rodeo, his final time as a school principal.

Our Mother Away from Home

Retirement beckons for this 70-year-old, who dreams of fishing and doing crossword puzzles and playing with his grandkids, who all lived in ocean cities nearby. A widower, his life is wrapped lovingly around his family.

As an English teacher, Cassie taught one class each year, not only to keep in touch with students but also to keep up with her subject in the event that an increase in student enrollment required assigning an extra teacher. Her favorite was English IV, when she taught *Hamlet.*

She got a text from her best friend Ellie Scanlon, who was toiling in the front office, organizing the piles of mail that had accumulated during the summer:

The General needs to see you ASAP.

Great, thought Cassie. I have no idea what's up.

The "General's" real name was Constance Daniels, Bennington's principal, who ran the office like she was a decorated general in the United States Army, though she was never in the military. No one called her Connie...heaven forbid.   She was formal and stern, except when she wanted something from you. In that case, she was syrupy sweet, which obviously was a pretense, as it didn't fit her personality one iota.

The teachers and staff used the moniker behind Constance's back. However, Cassie was sure that Constance knew about it, because she knew *everything* that happened at Bennington.

Four years ago, Constance arrived at Bennington, and since then she has been a total enigma to the faculty and staff. Was she married? No sign of a ring. Where did she come from? She hadn't divulged that. What kind of experience in education did she have? To say that she was a private person was an understatement. Only a select few at the school district knew the particulars, Cassie figured.

Ellie greeted Cassie when she entered the pristine front office, decorated in plaques dedicated to award-winning sports programs and educational extracurricular activities such as Academic Decathlon and Model United Nations. Model planes were everywhere: as awards, as props, some dropped from the ceiling. The school colors of blue and silver shone proudly in the displays.

"What's going on?" Cassie's eyebrows rose with the question.

"Sorry. Don't know." Ellie's cluelessness was uncharacteristic. Just like her boss, Ellie had a pulse on the comings and goings at Bennington. She shook her head, her short, blonde hair bobbing back and forth, and cast a look toward the General's closed door. Ellie was cute and perky, the perfect person to greet visitors when they arrived in the office.

"I'll tell Ms. Daniels that you're here, Miss Greenwood!" she said. They both chuckled.

"Cassandra!" the General exclaimed as she bounded out of her door, her arms flung wide. "I trust that you had a wonderful summer!" Yup, the syrup was thick as molasses. "Come right in," she gestured to her office, and closed the door when both were inside and out of Ellie's earshot.

Our Mother Away from Home

The General was a stout woman of five feet two, with no-nonsense hair cut bluntly below her ears. Grey hairs were infiltrating the natural brown ones slowly, showing her age of 55. She didn't walk, but rather marched, her steps deliberate and solid. Indeed, she did resemble a general.

Ellie had invented the nickname, but she would neither confirm nor deny that fact if prodded.

Just as no one addressed Constance as Connie, the opposite applied to Cassie. Not even her parents called her Cassandra. Ever! Why the General chose to do so was beyond Cassie, who guessed that it was a part of her formal nature.

The General wasted no time in blurting out her purpose for this little meeting before their rear ends hit the cushions of their twin couches.

"Our numbers in English are excellent this year, as far as the student-to-teacher ratio is concerned," she began. "I will need you to teach in the Physical Education and Health Department instead."

Wait! What? The idea made Cassie immediately wince. She shot up in shock, standing before the General's desk, her mouth agape, her hands on her hips.

"But, Constance, my degree is in English! You know, 'to be or not to be' and 'out, damned spot.'" Cassie quoted *Hamlet* and *Macbeth*, respectively. How she loved her Will Shakespeare.

"Now, Cassandra," the General interrupted. "Because of strict budgetary reasons, we cannot bring in a new teacher for just one class. You are contracted to teach exactly one class, and our needs are in the Physical Education and Health Department this year."

She continued, "You will be taking over for Pam Roland, who decided not to return to school after giving birth to her son Preston in July."

Cassie calmed down momentarily, thinking that a physical education class could be kind of fun. She imagined games and races and lessons on health and wellness.

"You will be teaching sex education the first semester, and health and safety the second semester," the General stated firmly. The syrup part of the meeting melted into the couch cushions, replaced with her formality. "You will have 20 sophomores."

What?!! Cassie was accustomed to teaching juniors and seniors, even when she was just an English teacher. Sophomores were just that—sophomoric!

According to the dictionary:

Sophomoric:

Adjective

Lacking in maturity, taste, or judgment

Conceited and overconfident of knowledge but poorly informed and immature

Cassie viewed sophomores as pimply, hyper, unfortunate creatures of the Earth. Freshman year was in the books, as were uncertainty, discomfort, and positioning at the bottom of the four-year totem pole. In their place were overly confident students who ruled the underclass sphere.

Was she just being a snob toward the underclassmen?

Speechless, Cassie took a seat. How could she complain about this arrangement? Her contract didn't specify in which discipline she would be needed. She had just been lucky that an English class was open every year the past four years, as she transitioned from teaching to administration. And she'd been lucky to avoid teaching freshmen and sophomores.

How would she do it?

Sex education was a million awkward moments ago.

Cassie vaguely remembered the cringe-worthy videotapes featuring body parts and their functions. Did those tapes still exist? In DVD form? Streaming on some service?

"Do you have any questions?" The General asked curtly, glancing at her watch. "If not, I have a conference call in five minutes with the superintendent."

"No," Cassie replied in a small voice.

"Thank you," the General said. "You should get your textbook tomorrow."

Our Mother Away from Home

"Greeeeaaat," Cassie sarcastically elongated the word, and exited the General's office.

Ellie stood up as Cassie flew through the door, and swiftly closed it.

"I'm teaching sex and health this year," Cassie blurted out, cutting to the chase. "To *sophomores*!" She spat out the word as if it were a curse cast on her by a wayward gypsy.

"Damn!" Ellie whispered. "When have you ever taught underclassmen? Or health?"

"Never!" exclaimed Cassie.

"Girlfriend, I think this calls for an emergency chardonnay," replied Ellie. "Meet me after school at the Pizza Project? I can be there by four."

"Awesome idea," said Cassie.

The Pizza Project was one of Cassie and Ellie's regular haunts. Because Ellie waited tables there all during high school, she was somewhat of a celebrity whenever she visited.

"Miss Ellie!" Bruno Bertolli, the owner, came running out from behind the counter to envelop her in a gigantic hug. Born in Sicily, he was a large man who loved his restaurant and everyone who happened by. He was a gentle giant, over six feet and about 250 pounds.

Despite his girth, Bruno had a certain grace about him, akin to a portly opera singer about to launch into an aria.

"How are you doing, *ciccino mio*?" He loved to call her the Italian equivalent of *my little friend*.

Ellie was deftly raised about a foot off the ground in Bruno's embrace. He then approached Cassie and did the same.

Today was Monday Madness, when the Project charged just 75 cents per slice—your choice of cheese or pepperoni. The crowds were crazy from 11-4, when the madness ended. Luckily, Cassie and Ellie were able to partake in a little bit of the Madness just after 4, getting the last two cheese slices available in the restaurant. And the pizza was *molto bene*! Yearly, the Pizza Project was at the top of the list of best Italian restaurants in the *Oakview Register*'s Book of Excellence.

"Do you know anything about current sex education practices?" Cassie asked Ellie as they chose a private table in a corner of the restaurant.

"Not a bit," Ellie confessed.

Ellie was somewhat of a Renaissance woman. She was taking online classes for her Bachelor's degree in business, a bit late to the party. Before she became an administrative assistant, Ellie was a hairdresser, a Pampered Chef party planner, and a sous chef at a French restaurant. Despite Ellie's younger age of 28 to Cassie's 32, Ellie relished new experiences wherever she encountered them.

"Do you think that I am being snobbish?" Cassie asked.

"No!" Ellie quietly protested. "You didn't sign up for this class! Let's just see how it goes." She wanted to reassure Cassie.

Their slices and wine arrived, and they dug in.

This was a real treat for Cassie, who normally didn't include cheesy goodness in her pretty strict diet. Oh, well. There is always running, part of her active lifestyle since high school.

For the next hour, the ladies caught up on much-missed gossip and the latest news. Ellie gave a vivid description of the cute new biology teacher, Sam Robbins. Dark hair, dark eyes, very tanned skin. He sounded mysterious but was very approachable, according to Ellie.

Cassie discussed her crazy busy schedule for September. Then it was time to end their happy hour, as Ellie had homework and Cassie continued to slog through the emails that had accumulated since she left for her abbreviated summer vacation three weeks earlier.

"*Ciao*, ladies!" Bruno bellowed as they left. "Until next time!"

Bruno has been happily married for 40 years to Maria, who runs the Pizza Project #2. They have five children and 10 grandchildren, Bruno's *bambinos*.

Our Mother Away from Home

Thursday came, and the Jets gleefully filled the noisy halls of Bennington, sporting suntans and smiles, anxious to see their pals again. Both today and Friday would be half-days, giving everyone a chance to ease in to the year. The class schedule would be Blocks 1-4 on Thursday, 5-8 on Friday. Luckily, Health I was Block 5, so Cassie had a free day.

One of her tasks was to review September's student activities. The ASB luncheon was scheduled for next Monday, the Welcome (Back) Dance for the next Friday, the ASB/faculty luncheon during the following week. School pictures were sprinkled in between. And the transfer students' luncheon paired a seasoned Jet with a newbie Jet on the 15th.

Note to self: Meet with the school's yearbook adviser, Tina Caldwell, regarding photo coverage for these events. She would email her ASAP.

Ellie popped in to deliver Cassie's textbook, *Health and Sex Education*. The plain title said it all. She was so screwed.

"Buck up, BFF!" chirped Ellie. She also delivered a surprise Iced Guava Passionfruit Drink from Starbucks, Cassie's favorite.

"Aw, thanks!" said Cassie.

"The wall of love is looking great!" Ellie commented about the myriad mementos displayed on the giant corkboard mounted in the wall behind Cassie's desk. Ellie named it that because it was rife with notes from students, picture Christmas cards, and other memorabilia from the past four years. Pictures from ASB camp and dances detailed the highlights of Cassie's tenure as Activities Director. There was even an invitation to a baby shower for a student who graduated two years ago.

"Hey," said Ellie. "Let's play the roster game."

Ellie made up the roster game when she and Cassie became friends at the beginning of Ellie's first year at Bennington. The two studied Cassie's roster, prognosticating about the students' personalities, based totally on their names.

Cassie passed her 20-person roster on to Ellie.

"Okay," said Ellie. "Sophia Bennington. Thinking this is the granddaughter of the founder of the school. Interesting."

Ellie continued, "Declan McIntosh, definitely an Irish kid."

And there was January Propst, a female. "That is the first kid I have had who is named after a month," said Cassie. She wondered what prompted her parents to name her January.

Maybe she was named after actress January Jones.

"Porter Sheffield," said Ellie. "That is a great name! Wonder what he is like. I hope he isn't stuck up."

This little exercise was just what Cassie needed, and Ellie was pleased. She accomplished what she set out to do: distract Cassie.

Our Mother Away from Home

"Hey," said Cassie, "Fill me in on the new teachers and staff." Ellie would have the lowdown on the new Bennington employees who were hired during Cassie's mini-vacation by the General and Tom Reynolds, Assistant Principal of Curriculum.

"Okay, the new science teacher, yummy Sam, used to work at an aquarium that partnered with a middle school nearby. Kind of what you will have at Marina Shores."

She continued, "Libby Jackson is a new Spanish teacher, and Neil Williams is taking over the other classes that Pam Roland taught. He is part-time. And our new librarian, Janet Parker, is an older person, but seems caught up on the latest technology. That is a good thing."

On Friday, Cassie met the Block Five 20. As predicted, they were bouncing around the classroom upon their noisy entrance to Room 602.

At the sound of the bell, Cassie addressed them: "Ladies and gentlemen, welcome to Health Education. I am Miss Greenwood. This year, we will be covering sex education the first semester and health and safety the second semester. I will provide your textbooks when I see you on Tuesday." At the mention of sex education, there were tons of snickers. Sophomoric!

Cassie showed a Keynote slide show about her life, as was her practice since her first year of teaching. Its contents changed slightly over the years. Her parents' passing was one memorable change to the Keynote.

Our Mother Away from Home

To get the students to know one another, Cassie paired them up and they interviewed their new pals. Each student was asked five questions by their interviewers. The only rule was that those questions could not elicit yes or no answers. To make it interesting, Cassie didn't offer any direction regarding the questions.

Ten minutes later, the Block Five 20 introduced their new friends. The questions had run the gamut from favorite color to pets to how they spent their summer vacation. A few were asked what their favorite class was during freshman year.   Jenny Cooper was asked what activities she was looking forward to for her sophomore year. Games, dances, the school newspaper (the *Aviator*) and Art Club were her answers.

As if on cue, the bell rang right after the last pair wrapped up.

"Have a nice weekend!" Cassie called out as everyone scrambled to pack up and leave.

She returned to her office and emailed the yearbook adviser to set up a meeting regarding upcoming activities. Then she called Ransom Entertainment, confirming the DJ for the Welcome (Back) Dance.

As Activities Director, Cassie had to plan dances many months in advance, whether they were held on campus or at hotels, such as with Homecoming, the Sweetheart Dance, and Prom. And Ransom always came through with great DJs. The administrative assistant at Ransom confirmed the DJ, so Cassie was all set. The Welcome (Back) Dance would be held in the Bennington gym.

15

Our Mother Away from Home

At 5:00, Cassie left campus after a week that seemed like a month. Exhausted, she decided to ditch her Nikes and skip the run. Instead, she drove to a nearby park with her journal and sat and scribbled her thoughts about the current life and times of Cassandra Marie Greenwood.

The weekend went by quickly, punctuated by usual chores and preparing for the upcoming week. Even though she was an administrator, Cassie still had to submit lesson plans to Tom Reynolds. Sunday was dedicated to relaxation, which would commence after Cassie's run and continue until bedtime. Bingeing Netflix, eating take-out from California Pizza Kitchen, and reading emails were the highlights of the day.

The first complete week of school was in full swing at busy Bennington. The ASB was feted with a special lunch over each of the two lunch periods on Monday, provided by the Pizza Project at a much-reduced cost.

Bruno loved the publicity that these lunches garnered for his restaurant. He even made a larger-than-life appearance during upper lunch with the juniors and seniors, schmoozing the crowd like he was a candidate running for mayor of Oakview. Come to think of it, Bruno would be a *great* mayor of Oakview. Too bad the present mayor, Max Dunlap, was in his 30's and in for the long haul.

Cassie was the emcee of a drawing held during both lunch periods; gift cards showcased many local businesses, including the Pizza Project. She was very happy with the convivial exchange among the ASB students, who were led by ASB President Zack Anderson.

She emceed a second drawing during lower lunch.

Friday was an extremely long day. Cassie stayed at school until the dance was to start, and changed to casual clothes and tennis shoes.

At 3:00, she met with Tina Caldwell, a stunning, statuesque, almost-too-thin yearbook adviser who moonlighted as a hand model. Tina's nose was permanently planted in the air, and her thick mane of red hair shone and swayed as she walked.

Cassie always laughed when she recalled her first meeting with Tina.

"I don't shake hands," Tina declared, her first words to Cassie. "My hands are insured because I work as a hand model in my spare time." She held up her hands as if to prove her statement correct, and as if she were, inexplicably, doing jazz hands.

Cassie wondered what kind of regimen Tina followed in caring for her insured hands. They were flawless. One day, she would have the gumption to ask her where her hands have been. Commercials? Magazines? You never know. And what does it cost to insure hands?

She pictured Tina living alone in an apartment with just lettuce and Smart Water in the refrigerator, and with a hairless cat whose claws were painted white. She was equal parts beauty and mystery.

Our Mother Away from Home

"Okay," began Cassie, sloughing off her mental musings. "Please fill me in on your yearbook deadlines."

"Our deadlines are November 15, January 15, March 15 and April 15," she said, glancing at the contract with Harvard Yearbooks that they both signed last spring with yearbook representative Jonathan Bennett looking on. "The book will arrive by the end of May. I will run all pages by you."

Yeah, you'd better do that, thought Cassie.

"I appreciate that," she said.

One of Cassie's many jobs was to oversee the yearbook pages and give her stamp of approval on the production. She had a wary eye, always looking for hand signals in pictures and typos in copy.

The ladies discussed photo coverage for upcoming activities, beginning with tonight's dance. Ransom partnered with Albert Jones Photography, which supplied activity photos as a bonus for shooting the seniors' portraits.

After the meeting, Cassie briskly walked the students' track in the hours in between school and the dance, and ate her Subway turkey and provolone sandwich at her desk for dinner.

The gym had been decorated after school by the Senior Class Officers. The balloons, jumbo map of Hawaii, and multi-colored leis reflected the "Hawaiian Hotspot" theme. There was a photo station, decked out with leis, sunglasses, and hats. Students were asked to dress in tropical clothing for the occasion.

She scanned the gym, ready to welcome the dancing Jets to the festive atmosphere.

She glanced over to the DJ set-up, but the guy who would spin the tunes didn't look familiar. Must be a new DJ, she thought.

As she got closer to this new guy, she thought that he did look familiar. But from where?

"Hi," she said, "I am Activities Director Cassie Greenwood. Welcome to Bennie," she extended her hand in greeting.

"Pete Patterson," he said, reaching forward and closing his hand over hers.

Cassie felt herself blush as she squeezed her hand into his. What a hunk! She was reminded of the old '60s band, the Beach Boys, as she gazed over his deep tan, blonde hair, and dreamy blue eyes. She continued to size him up: six feet, toned, looking like a model in his dark T-shirt and jeans.

He *could* be a Beach Boy.

"I am sorry, but you look familiar," Cassie confessed.

"I get that all the time," he laughed. "I am the morning drive DJ on KFUNN 105.7, Monday through Friday, so you might have seen me on billboards for the station. I go by DJ PJ Panda."

"Of course!" Cassie exclaimed. "And you work for Ransom as well?"

"Yes, I have, on occasion," said Pete. "When they get in a bind, I'm their man."

"Okay," said Cassie. "Glad to have you on board, Pete. Can I get you a bottle of water or some snacks?"

"Just some water, thanks.   I just had dinner at the Pizza Project. Do you know that place? That was the best pizza I have ever had!"

"Yes, I am very familiar with it," Cassie smiled. "As a matter of fact, the Pizza Project team fed my ASB kids on Monday. Bruno, the owner, paid a visit."

"Is he the big dude?" Pete reached his hand skyward, indicating Bruno's enormous height.

"Yes," confirmed Cassie. "He gives great hugs."

"I can imagine," Pete snickered.

At 7:00, the kids filed in, looking great in their Hawaiian garb. Pete had the latest tunes already booming through the gym to officially kick off the dance. The kids were in great spirits and danced the night away.

The General dropped by to check up on the festivities, and the head of the deans, Marco Cordova, kept a watchful eye on the dancing and general tomfoolery. No one seemed out of line, a miracle in Cassie's eyes.

Our Mother Away from Home

By 10:00, it was time to call it a night. Pete played one last song, "Bennie and the Jets," and the kids started jumping up and down when it blasted over the gym.

Good, thought Cassie. The other DJs clued Pete in on the non-negotiable closing song.

Just as they entered the gym, the kids exited en masse, chatting away and, for some, romantically holding hands for the first time as a pair.

"Thanks so much, Pete," Cassie ventured over when he was packing up his equipment.

"Glad to help."

"So, do you also teach?" Pete was eager to enter into a conversation with Cassie. He liked the way she looked, filling her jeans nicely with her cute curves. She reminded him of a pixie, light on her feet, feathery, and lively.

"I usually teach one class each year, when the need arises. It is usually an English class, which was my undergrad major, but this year I am teaching health and sex education," she explained. "Not really happy about that."

They talked incessantly while the next two hours flew by. The night cleaning crew did its thing, and ASB members returned the decorations to Cassie's office. Long ago, Pete had finished his packing. Now it was just the two of them seated side by side in the bleachers, drinking water and eating the last of the snacks that were allocated for the party-goers.

Pete shared that he returned to the area two years ago when he accepted the gig at KFUNN. Previously, he worked as a DJ in Arizona, after graduating from the University of Arizona with a degree in arts and media. He attended Bennington's rival, Oakview High School, home of the Eagles. He played baseball in high school, but skipped it in college. Cassie wondered why their paths never crossed, especially since they both graduated the same year, and both were athletes. She told her athletic story.

"Yikes!" Cassie burst out as she glanced at her watch. "It's midnight! Time to go."

"I can't believe it!" Pete incredulously looked at his own watch.

"Hey," he said, "I have an idea. Why don't you pick two chapters of the sex ed portion of your book, and I will have my mom come in and be a guest speaker. She is a labor and delivery nurse who teaches nursing at Walker College. She is retiring at the end of the semester, and has some flexibility in her schedule. By the way, her name is Patsy."

"OMG!" yelled Cassie, throwing her arms around Pete's neck, and came in for a hug. "That would be sooo great." She momentarily forgot that he was practically a stranger, and removed her arms from said neck.

She continued, "Okay, I know right off the bat that the chapter titled 'What Is Sex?' is one that I would gladly hand off to her. I have dreaded this chapter. Please take my contact information."

With that, they both exchanged phone numbers and emails.

Before Pete left, he turned to Cassie.

"Hey, what kind of music do you like?"

"Anything but the '80s, with the exception of Heart. I'll pass on those groups like Aha and Soft Cell, who seemed to be one-hit wonders. Just thinking of that era evokes strange images of huge, androgynous hair and monstrous shoulder pads!"

Pete just laughed.

Cassie left school feeling charged, despite the early-morning hour. Clearly, this was the bright light that she needed in the gloom of the past week. Patsy Patterson would be her hero. Boy, that family really loves alliteration.

She couldn't wait to tell Ellie. She texted her when she got home.

Meet me at Café California this morning? Got some great info to share with you.

A few minutes later, Ellie replied.

How about 9? Need to walk Dino.

Great!!! See ya then!

Dino was Ellie's dog, a mixture of basenji and corgi. He was her constant companion, except when she went in to work. Tried as she might, she couldn't figure out how to smuggle Dino into the front office during working hours, even though he was only an eight-pound puppy.

Since she was a girl, Ellie had been fascinated with paleontology; thus was the source of her dog's name.

Cassie entered Café California promptly at 9, feeling grateful for Patsy Patterson. And Pete, for that matter.

"Okay, girlfriend, spill it!" Ellie was desperate for news, and seemed to revel in it. Maybe her next job would be in journalism.

Cassie told her everything about the dance, about Pete, and his brilliant idea about incorporating his mother's expertise into her curriculum.

"Is he cute?" Of course, that would be of paramount importance in Ellie's mind.

"Yes! He is a blond, blue-eyed hunk of a guy!"

"I think you're in trouble!" Ellie chirped.

Over scones and pumpkin spice lattes, the ladies pondered the latest developments. Cassie admitted that she looked forward to seeing Pete again in some capacity.

Cassie and Ellie were a great team when it came to hashing things out.

The weekend was a repeat of last weekend: chores, lesson plans, Netflix. However, on Friday night, the Jet football team played its first game of the season, beating Camden Academy, 14-0. Cassie was, as usual, planted on the field as a supervisor. She decided to go up into the stands to watch the lavish halftime show, featuring the band, cheerleaders, and song leaders. The field was resplendent in blue and silver, which seemed to pop off the grass. What a sight, she thought.

On Sunday night, Cassie got a call from Patsy Patterson. They chatted about the school schedule, and decided that Patsy would come in October 1st to discuss the sex chapter.

"You cannot believe how grateful I am," said Cassie. "I don't even know you, but I am so thankful for your generosity."

"Oh, honey!" said Patsy. "I understand that this was thrust upon you. I am just glad to take over. I have been around sophomores before!"

Cassie promised to get a teacher's copy of the textbook the next week.

She texted Pete after the phone call.

Your mom sounds like such a lovely lady!

He responded.

Yes, she is. She was widowed when my father died at 50 from a heart attack. She raised three boys and did a great job.

Cassie's enthusiasm was nearly palpable.

Man, I can't wait to meet her! Just was wondering if you want to get together for a drink or coffee. I can give you a copy of the textbook for your mom.

Pete devised a plan.

How about that pizza place tomorrow? There were posters about something happening on Mondays.

Great! Yes, Monday Madness. Cheap slices on Mondays. How is 4:00?

Sounds good!

Because Pete worked the 6-10 a.m. shift at KFUNN, he usually had a late-morning nap. He'd be good to go by 4. Cassie was just hoping that there would be some Madness left over for them.

She had to admit that she usually didn't tune in to KFUNN, which offered oldies in addition to current tunes. "From the '70s and '80s to today, KFUNN plays all the best hits," is their tagline. Conversely, she listened to Ryan Seacrest on KIIS FM, 102.7.

Her curiosity piqued as she decided to check out "DJ PJ Panda."

"Hey, everyone, it's DJ PJ, your morning drive man at KFUNN. It's now 6:30, and after this two-minute commercial, we'll have 60 minutes of nonstop music," said Pete. "We'll begin with 'Alone' by Heart."

Cassie was bummed, but happy. She had to leave by 7:00, and she wanted to hear more of Pete. And she loved that he played a Heart song. A longer listen would have to wait for another morning.

Our Mother Away from Home

On Monday, the administration gathered for its usual weekly meeting, with Constance in charge and Ellie playing scribe.

Tom Reynolds reported on the Advanced Placement scores from the summer, which were nearly perfect for AP Studio Art, AP English Language, and AP Spanish Culture. Constance beamed, as if she had a personal hand in the AP success. Tom was her right-hand man, a bachelor of 40, destined to move up in administration at some point.

Christine Walker, the Assistant Principal of Faculty and Staff, updated the new-hire list, which included someone new in the facilities department. Christine loved her job. She especially loved observing the teachers, where she always learned something new. Married to Bill, an accountant, they had two little girls, ages 5 and 6.

Cassie discussed the Welcome (Back) Dance, and gave a preview of the Homecoming festivities that would take place the week of October 15.

Satisfied, Constance called an end to the meeting in mid-morning.

"Thank you, everyone, for your contributions." Constance actually seemed sincerely grateful. Again, this mystery woman perplexed Cassie as she exited the conference room.

The ASB and faculty/staff luncheon was another success for Cassie that afternoon. The faculty and staff members often told her that their ASB lunch buddies became favorites of theirs. Some even kept in touch with the students, and gave them presents for their birthdays and Christmas.

Once again, Cassie was the emcee, but the raffle she hosted had a lot more prizes. The top prize was a $50.00 gift card to the Oakview Mall.

By 4:00, Cassie arrived at the Pizza Project, and spied Pete through the door. She took a moment to revel in the sight of him. So easy on the eyes, so handsome. She wondered what it would be like to kiss him. Or, to do other things with him. Suddenly, her girl parts came to life.

"Hi, Cassie," Pete stood up and greeted her. Points for Pete! Cassie had a great appreciation for gentlemen.

"Hey, Pete," replied Cassie.

Bruno was busy with the last-minute Madness crowd. But he lit up when Pete and Cassie approached the counter. Cassie introduced Pete to Bruno.

"Good to see you two!" he said. "But, I am sorry that we just ran out of slices. Would you like to order a mini or small pie?"

They decided on a mini pepperoni, a salad, and two beers.

"I tuned in to KFUNN this morning," Cassie confessed. "You were just going to commercial before 60 minutes of music."

"Yeah, we do that every morning about that time," Pete said. "It calms people on their commute to work."

That made total sense. Put the listeners in a good mood to start their day.

He added, "You missed my interview with Gina Toledo of Primavera, the long-running restaurant. It has been in her family for 60 years. She literally grew up in that restaurant, and now owns it."

"Oh, I love that place! Shhh!!! Maybe I shouldn't be saying that in the house of Bruno!" she laughed. She also loved the fact that the restaurant was within walking distance of her house.

"Gina sent over a gift card as a thank-you gift," said Pete. "Maybe we can go there next time."

Cassie smiled. *Next time* sounded so nice coming off the lips of the dreamy guy sitting next to her. He looked especially cute in jeans and a flannel shirt.

"I would love that!" she said. "I always order the same thing: Penne Sicily. Penne with light cream sauce, chicken, mushrooms, and pancetta. It is heavenly."

Each time Cassie saw Pete, she memorized little things about him.   Like the way his blue eyes crinkled at the edges when he laughed. Or when he sensuously licked his lips after taking a swig of beer.

It reminded her of that Gloria Estefan song, "I See Your Smile," where the singer admires and memorizes someone's attributes.

I think Ellie's right, thought Cassie. I *am* in trouble.

As with their post-dance visit in the gym, time flew. Cassie handed over a teacher's edition of her textbook that she pilfered from the bookstore manager at Bennie, after some sweet talk and a big *pretty please*.

Unable to resist, Pete opened up the book and went straight to "What Is Sex?"

She winced.

"Oh, boy!" He scanned the illustrations. "I can see why you wanted to avoid this chapter. Trust Mom. She can hit on the basics and will do a great job."

Pete was quickly becoming enamored with this little pixie and her flowery, feminine clothing. Today, she chose a green sundress with daisies. Adorable! She would never admit to anyone—except maybe Ellie--that she owned 28 dresses. Yes, one more than the title of the Katherine Heigl movie.

They said their goodbyes, and Cassie went home to walk, not run, her first time getting exercise in three days. And she felt it later, soaking in a bubbly tub before bedtime.

The next day, the General marched into Cassie's office.

Cassie's head jerked up.

"Hello, Cassandra," chirped the General. "How was the Welcome (Back) Dance?"

"It was great. Marco confirmed that the students all behaved, and I saw no evidence that showed otherwise."

Wait for it, Cassie thought.

"Oh, really?" the General took a step closer to Cassie's desk. "I just got a call from a parent who said that there was a lot of vaping going on in the restrooms during the dance."

Bingo! There it is!

"Marco and his deans were in and out of the restrooms all night long." Cassie went into defensive mode. "I don't want to call the parent a liar, but I strongly disagree."

"I understand," said the General sternly. "Just make sure that this doesn't happen again." With that, she marched out.

But it **didn't happen**!!! What a bitch! Why does she hate me so much?

Trying to calm down, Cassie went back to work.

She reflected on the Block Five 20, which was turning out to be a very nice group of kids. Sophia Bennington was a humble little thing, surprisingly. She always aimed to please. Declan McIntosh was quickly morphing into the class clown. Even to his face, Cassie called him a leprechaun. He loved it. January Propst, a blonde beauty and a cheerleader, was, indeed, named after January Jones. And Porter Sheffield was a scrawny guy who never spoke up in class, and always kept to himself. Cassie decided to plan a group activity for next class, to get Porter to interact with his peers.

Thus far, the textbook appeared innocuous. Mostly, the content delved into our bodies, ourselves. Cassie talked a lot about body image, and showed some YouTube videos about the subject. The students asked questions about eating disorders, and Cassie thought that diversion must have been on the forefront of some of their minds.

Cassie caught up with Ellie over late-afternoon coffees in the front office.

"So," began Ellie, "How is it going with the dream DJ?"

"Oh, Ellie!" exclaimed Cassie, "You were right! I *am* in trouble!"

"I knew it!" Ellie plopped two sugar cubes into her coffee. This certainly wasn't Starbucks. "I just have a sixth sense when it comes to romance!"

The pals rehashed the Pizza Project date, and Pete's reaction to the sex ed book. Ellie confessed that she was setting her sights on yummy Sam, who wasn't married or involved presently. With her access to school records and her constant Facebook presence, Ellie's sleuthing skills were sharpened. She came to the conclusion that Sam was single and ready to mingle.

The transfer student luncheon marked the last luncheon for the beginning of this semester for Cassie. The students came from across the United States, China, Korea,

and everywhere in between. All were involved in the luncheon, which included interactive games such as bingo and, for the athletically inclined, horse in basketball.

For the luncheon, Cassie decided to order food from Primavera, and Gina, the owner, paid a visit. Unlike Bruno, the motherly Gina donned her green apron with the Italian flag embroidered at the top, and helped to bus tables. A tall blonde with curly hair always in a ponytail, she went from table to table with a trash can on wheels. It almost looked as if she was doing lunch detention! She moved like she did in her restaurant—zip, zip, zip!

Later in the week, Cassie tuned in to Pete's show one morning.

He was chatting about schools re-opening, and included a shout-out to teachers.

"Hello, everyone!" he said after a song ended. "I just wanted to give a shout-out to all of the teachers out there who are getting back to business after summer vacation. I especially want to say hi to someone in the front office at Bennington High School, who makes a lot of things happen with her mad organizational skills."

Is that me? Cassie wondered. I make things happen?

With a bounce in her step, Cassie grabbed her purse and backpack, and left her house.

Because of their busy schedules, Cassie and Pete didn't see each other for a few weeks. He was slated to broadcast from the California State Fair in San Diego the next week, and she tuned in a few days to listen to all of his adventures: eating samples from some fried food groups-- pickles, Oreos, and butter; feeding an alpaca; riding on the tilt-a-whirl. What a sweet gig!

Pete interviewed the president of the Fair, Reggie Walters, whose sole job all year revolved around this 21-day stint. He told Pete about all of the displays—including a 200-pound pumpkin—and the crowning of Miss California State Fair on the last day of the festivities.

There were the new rides, and, of course, new fried offerings, such as the bacon-wrapped tater puffs and tacos on a stick. Reggie shared that the fried-chicken-stuffed glazed donut was his perennial favorite. Pete imagined it was delicious, though he had his fill of deep fried anything by the end of the week.

Chelsea Smithson was crowned Miss California State Fair. A senior at Torrey Pines High School in San Diego, Chelsea aspired to be a dentist. She was accepted to the University of San Diego, and hoped to get into the Herman Ostrow School of Dentistry at the University of Southern California. Pediatric dentistry would be her specialty.

"What does the crown mean to you?" Pete asked Chelsea.

"Pete, I have such fond memories of coming to the Fair with my family since I was a little girl, even though my mom sacrificed at times to get us here," said Chelsea, a stunning brunette with a cascade of curls that fell to her waist. "I always dreamed of being crowned Miss California

State Fair, and serving as a role model to young girls and a wonderful representative of the city of San Diego. I will wear my crown proudly."

"Why pediatric dentistry?" Pete was curious.

"I grew up with a single mother who had four kids," explained Chelsea. "At times, my mom took on two jobs, and, as I was the oldest, I had to babysit my siblings. I have a soft spot for children, so I want to focus on them in my career."

Cassie texted Pete shortly thereafter.

Great interview with Miss Cali Fair!

He replied an hour later.

Thanks! She was so poised and smart and driven. I predict a stellar future for her.

September rolled along, and Cassie looked forward to Patsy Patterson's appearance on October 1st.

The Block Five 20 had their first test, on the human anatomy. Cassie had given them silhouettes of the male and female bodies, and the students were to mark the different parts. Cassie was happy that their scores were outstanding. So far, so good with the Block Five 20.

"Miss Greenwood?" asked Declan McIntosh one day, as he bounded out of his seat. "Do you have a boyfriend?"
Talk about apropos of nothing. The class was discussing the next chapter of the textbook, "A Healthy Lifestyle."

Cassie was taken aback. She rarely shared tidbits of her personal life with her students. The Keynote on the first day of school was the most revealing.

"Why, Declan," she said to the class clown, "that is a very personal question. I will just say that I have many friends, male and female."

Declan, defeated, sat right back down.

Cue the bell.

And, with the chimes, September became a memory.

Chapter Two - October

October was bathed in the rustic colors of fall—burnt orange and scarlet and maize—as the glorious city of Oakview displayed itself in all of its autumnal splendor. No wonder it was known as the "City of 1,000 Oaks."

Sweaters appeared out of storage, and the crisp days grew shorter. At Bennington, students hung out among the fallen leaves and enjoyed the fiery sunsets across the football, soccer, and baseball fields. With Homecoming just a few weeks away, students were turning crafty in their bid for dates. One boy covered his would-be date's car with myriad sticky notes, each one posing a question: *Homecoming?* Flowers appeared everywhere; it looked like Wanda from Wanda's Flowers and Gifts had taken up residence among the Jets.

This was Cassie's favorite time of the year, as the month culminated in her favorite holiday, Halloween.

The students had settled into the routine of a new school year, which, so far, suffered few snafus. A chill in the air welcomed fans to Friday nights in the Jets Stadium, as the football team continued its winning streak, now 4-0. Life was good.

On October 1st, Cassie went outside of the front office in anticipation of Patsy Patterson's arrival before Block Five. She was shocked when a woman in a bright-pink helmet pulled her three-wheeled bicycle into a visitor parking spot. OMG! She had seen this woman many times around town and always chuckled when she saw her: a short, compact, blonde woman, presumably in her 60's, who skillfully commandeered the vehicle and always, always sported her helmet.

There was no shaking of hands with Patsy Patterson. Like a miniature female version of Bruno, she scooped up Cassie into a gigantic hug and made her feel so welcomed. And, unlike Bruno, she was all of about 5 feet 2 and 100 pounds.

"My dear!" exclaimed Patsy. "It is so great to meet you!"

"Oh, Mrs. Patterson!" responded Cassie. "You don't know what this means to me."

Patsy placed a hand on Cassie's shoulder. "Call me Patsy, and leave it all to me."

With that, Cassie slowly let her tense body melt in relaxation when she heard Patsy's comforting words.

I know that I have a Bennington sweatshirt for this woman, Cassie thought, but I really need to give her something more.

As previously decided, she would introduce Patsy to the class, and then quietly leave until the end of the period.

Our Mother Away from Home

"Class, this is Mrs. Patterson. She will be our guest speaker for today. Please be respectful and listen to her lesson. And, make sure that you ask any questions that arise."

"Hello, everyone. I am a labor and delivery nurse. Does anyone know what that means?"

Sophia Bennington's hand shot up.

"Yes, honey," said Patsy.

"You are a nurse who helps deliver babies." Sophia was rather proud of herself.

"That is exactly right. And I am a nurse who teaches beginning nurses at Walker College."

As Patsy began to describe her job, Cassie slipped away. She took coffee to Ellie, plopped down, and reveled in the stolen moments.

At the end of the period, Cassie quietly reentered her classroom. The students were enwrapped in Patsy's explanation of the sex chapter. They were so quiet, she was astounded. When the bell rang, almost everyone approached Patsy and said thank you.

Holy crap! These kids are really thankful.

"Patsy, this is unprecedented." Flummoxed, Cassie turned to her hero. "I am beyond grateful."

"Well, dear, we had a great time. Just let me know when you want me back."

Our Mother Away from Home

Patsy recounted the hour-long class, in which the students asked many questions about anatomy, reproduction, and sex. In her interaction with the students, Patsy discovered that Sophia's mother, Janet, works as a labor and delivery nurse at Oakview General Hospital. She actually knows Janet, as she occasionally works a shift in between teaching classes.

"Patsy!" yelped Cassie. "How will I get through the semester?"

"You will have to address the students' follow-up questions, and move on to the next chapter, which deals with choices about sex. Don't worry! The more you talk about sex, the easier it will be." Patsy reassured her.

Cassie handed Patsy a blue and silver gift bag holding a size small Bennington sweatshirt (Thank you, Pete, for the size info).

The ladies agreed that Patsy would reappear before Thanksgiving to cover sexually transmitted diseases. Have at it, thought Cassie.

The two hugged, and Cassie watched Patsy drive away in her three-wheeled bike until the pink helmet disappeared on the boulevard.

Thus began a very special friendship.

Pete was back from San Diego, and was gifted with two extra days off from the station manager, as thanks for covering the Fair. He decided to call Cassie.

"Hey!" he said. "What's up?"

"Hi! Just got back from a run."

Winded on this early Friday evening, she was downing water. "I need to do more of that. Kind of fell out of the habit since school started."

"I was wondering if you wanted to get together one of these days. How is your weekend looking?"

"This is a wide open weekend for me, a rarity during the school year. The football team has a bye tonight, and there are no school activities at all."

"Want to go on a hike tomorrow? The weather is supposed to be spectacular."

"Great idea! Do you want to pick me up?"

Pete got all of the details and picked up Cassie by 8 the next morning. It was, indeed, a magnificent day. They explored the zig-zag trails in Covington Canyon, and basked in the warmth. Cotton-candy clouds dotted the glorious landscape, and a light breeze delicately fanned the hikers.

Conversation came easily as the two new friends disclosed more of their lives.

Pete was once engaged to a fellow U of A student, a bio-chemistry major, named Andi. Their schedules were very demanding, as Pete started working nights at KPUB, a radio station smack in the middle of a pub. It was a fun, popular place, but Pete was still in school and he and Andi hardly ever saw each other. She was working days at a hospital and took classes at night. They quietly parted, vanquished by fate.

The move to KFUNN provided a fresh start for Pete, as he bade goodbye to KPUB and Andi, and hello, again, to his beloved hometown.

Cassie just had to ask why he went by DJ PJ Panda, of all names.

"When I was in Tucson, I had a sweet gig playing at openings of Panda Wok restaurants, which were popping up in the area. People always called me DJ Panda, and it stuck, so I attached it to DJ PJ," he explained. "My middle name is Joseph, by the way."

Cassie nostalgically mentioned her parents and divulged to Pete that she was adopted. She almost forgot about this little tidbit, as she had a wonderful life with a mother and father who thought she hung the moon. She never once felt adopted. Whether it was Girl Scouts, softball, or school plays, her parents were ever present.

It was sometimes a challenge for her coach father, but her mother Beverly, a homemaker, was a fixture at all of the activities. When her heart was torn in two by her high school boyfriend when he simultaneously trotted off to UCLA and broke up with her, they held her as she cried. She had no desire to find her birth parents.

Cassie realized toward the end of the hike that the topics that she and Pete shared were becoming more revealing, as they exposed their vulnerabilities to each other. Just like that, they were confiding in one another on a deeper level.

Exhausted and sunburnt, the pair called it a day in Covington Canyon. They decided to utilize Pete's gift card at Primavera that evening, after each napped post-hike.

Pete was back at Cassie's at 7:00.

"Wow, you look fantastic!" Pete exclaimed upon seeing Cassie in a bright electric-blue dress with matching earrings and sandals. She was rested and ready for a night out with Pete, their first evening date. Pete looked great, as well, in his khakis and button-down blue shirt. They looked like they were intentionally "twinning."

The pair decided to walk the four short blocks to the restaurant.

"Hey, you were right about your mom. She was wonderful with the students," Cassie commented. "Thank you so much for the suggestion."

"Great! I knew that it would all work out. Mom is a terrific teacher."

"What is with your alliterative names?" That was something that Cassie wanted to get to the bottom of.

"Well, my father's name was Prescott, but he went by Scotty. When my parents were dating, everyone thought it was so cute that Prescott Patterson was dating Patsy Pellington. They got married, and decided to keep up with the "P" names when they had kids. My brothers are Parker and Patrick, Park and Pat for short. They are both married, with two kids each."

Our Mother Away from Home

Primavera was bustling, as usual for a Saturday night. Gina was holding court at the check-in desk, and she warmly welcomed Pete and Cassie. The wait was a brief 10 minutes, as Gina was deft at moving guests in and out, kind of like a traffic director.

Cassie scanned the walls and decorations of the festive, colorful restaurant, which she has done many times. It always made her smile.

Checkered tablecloths, plastic clusters of grapes, and signed photos of important visitors completed the homey atmosphere.

Myriad celebrities visited Primavera—or, the Pri, as many called it over the years—from Richard Nixon in the early days of the restaurant, to, more recently, Brad Pitt and Quentin Tarantino, who were filming a portion of the movie *Once Upon a Time in Hollywood* down the street from Primavera.

The ambience reminded her of a haiku that she crafted in middle school:

"At Luigi's"
Cheery checkerboards
Dance red-white on tabletops
Ah! I smell pizza!

That little five-seven-five syllable ditty won her top prize at the city poetry contest for students aged 11-13 when Cassie was in the 8th grade. When you're 13, $25 is a fortune!

The Penne Sicily didn't disappoint. Pete loved it. The portions were so huge at the restaurant that they were able to split the entrée, and add a salad, and that was more than enough.

As Pete and Cassie were chowing down, Gina stopped by their table to inquire about their dining experience. They simultaneously posted two thumbs up, and she laughed.

Gina was a bit like Bruno, even though they were competitors: She loved her restaurant, and she loved her guests. She liked to do special things for her guests, like monthly wine tastings and, every other year, a tour of Italy in the summer.

Dessert was out of the question for these stuffed diners, even though the goody cart was so invitingly overloaded with tiramisu, cannoli, and biscotti.

They waved goodbye to Gina and headed out into the crisp autumn evening.

The citizens of Oakview were embracing the Halloween spirit in this second week of October, as pumpkins, skeletons, and other spooky adornments dotted Cassie's neighborhood. She loved the blow-up gigantic creatures, like the Dracula next door to her, and the green-skinned witch a few doors down.

Perhaps there was time for Cassie to begin decorating her house tomorrow. Sundays were chock full of chores; however, she'd make the time.

Somewhere between Primavera and Cassie's home, Pete grabbed Cassie's hand. She was so wrapped up in telling a story about the Block Five 20 inspecting plastic models of the human anatomy that she didn't even notice. When she realized what was happening, she just smiled. It seemed so natural to have her hand in his.

At her door, Cassie was the first to speak.

"Thank you so much for a wonderful day. I had such a great time from beginning to end." She added, "You are good company."

"Right back atcha! Let's get together again soon. Good night."

Pete's hands encircled Cassie's face, and, softly and sweetly, he kissed her lips. With that tender gesture, a line was crossed from friends to something more. Then he was gone.

Cassie closed the door behind her and pressed her body against it. With a deep sigh, she replayed the gentle porch-light kiss in her mind. It was simply perfect.

On Monday, the Block Five 20 gathered for the first time since Patsy's appearance.

Cassie braced herself for the inevitable sex questions. Thankfully, she had already had her coffee and was ready for the barrage.

"Now, class, how was your time with Mrs. Patterson?"

"She was a nice lady," said January. "I think we all felt comfortable asking her questions. She explained a lot in one class period."

Good answer, January.

Cassie had to ask. "Does anyone have any follow-up questions?"

"Is it true that you can get pregnant by having unprotected sex just once?" Of course, that would come from Declan.

"Yes, Declan, that is true. Just one time without protection can get a woman pregnant if she is ovulating." The class fell silent. The myth about one time was shattered in the minds of these young people who thought it wasn't possible.

Enough said. Time to move on.

The class began its discussion about peer pressure in the next chapter, "Making Choices about Sex."

Homecoming Week was upon Bennington, beginning October 15, and Cassie was at the ready to respond to any situation--negative or positive--that arose during the week. She was a combination of cruise director and commander-in-chief.

On Monday, the Homecoming Rally began when Constance approached the podium, her walk-up song, "Bennie and the Jets," blaring over the speakers. She thinks she *is* Bennie, Cassie thought. Hmmm...maybe she is.

Our Mother Away from Home

"Ladies and gentlemen, welcome to your Homecoming Rally. I am pleased to introduce Mayor Max Dunlap, who will officially kick off Homecoming Week."

Mayor Max shook Constance's hand and welcomed the students. He was a ginger, a bright shock of red hair jutting out of his head. Lean and lanky, his body reflected his daily swims in the Oakview Villas condo pool.

In addition to being mayor of Oakview, Max was an attorney specializing in family law.

"Hey, all you Jets!" Max began. "I am proud to say that I was once a student at Bennie, just like you. In fact, I was the ASB President during my senior year, and that was the start of my political career! Just like today, our mayor kicked off the Homecoming festivities, which is one of Bennington's cherished traditions. I hope that you enjoy all of the activities that have been planned for you by Ms. Greenwood and the ASB students."

As part of his mayoral appearance, Max was tasked with announcing the names of the Homecoming Court. Students had previously voted online for the court. Two girls in grades 9-11 were princesses. Five senior boys and five senior girls were princes and princesses. From that group, the Homecoming King and Queen were chosen.

Cassie delighted in the fact that January Propst was elected as a sophomore princess.

In a burst of fanfare, music blasted from the speakers, and Zack Anderson and Charlene Rodgers were crowned the royal couple. ASB Officers presented roses to the girls, and an Albert Jones photographer captured all of the merriment.

Our Mother Away from Home

Ellie once called Zack and his girlfriend, Lexi Cassidy, "clichés on a stick" because, stereotypically speaking, she is a cheerleader and he is a captain of the football team.

However, there was more to this duo than the nicknames and what met the eye. A senior, Zack would soon sign a letter of intent to Stanford, a football scholarship on his horizon. Lexi, a junior, had hopes of joining him in two years. Maybe she would earn a spot as a Cardinal cheerleader. Both were beyond-4.0-grade-point-average students.

Ellie was sorry to have misjudged the two.

Max crowned Charlene queen and, raising up his arms skyward, cried out, "Bennington, it is officially Homecoming Week!" The Jets went nuts, screaming with joy. Cue the music.

The mayor came out as gay during his campaign; his platform was equality for all. It was as if his disclosure cemented his place in Oakview politics, as his popularity soared upon the declaration. Word on the street is that he is dating the manager of Oakview First Bank, Harley Keffer. I hope Max is happy, Cassie thought. What a nice guy.

The week was sprinkled with fun activities, including a Bennington trivia contest that pitted the teachers against students from every class. Cassie had entrusted the Senior Class Officers with creating the questions.

Lots of fun facts emerged from the contest. For example, Lionel Bennington, one of the founding fathers of the school, appeared in the 1960s television show *The Dating Game,* and ended up marrying his date, Lisa Browning.

Our Mother Away from Home

It seemed that Lisa was a socialite whose family fortune was in oil. Lionel was a perfect match, as he came from money too. His family fortune was in real estate; that explained his involvement with the building of the campus. His family's storied philanthropic history in Oakview was rewarded with the acquisition of the school name.

The students won the contest, in a surprising twist. Cassie provided the victors gift cards for McDonald's.

On Friday night, the Homecoming Court arrived at Jets Stadium in convertibles, the princesses decked in blue dresses, Charlene in a white dress, and the guys in black tuxedos with blue dress shirts.

The evening was electrifying, as the stands were overflowing with Jets past and present. The court appeared on the field after the team's halftime exit, and one of the booth announcers introduced them. Sadly, the Jets suffered their first loss of the season, to Oakview, 7-3.

Oh, great, thought Cassie. Pete would be capitalizing on that little victory, gloating and donning an Eagles T-shirt. It was just too bad that the first defeat of the season fell on Homecoming.

Pete said nothing when she saw him next; he just ignored the topic. More points for gentleman Pete.

From the field, Cassie waved to Ellie, who was one of the last fans to exit the stadium. "See you tomorrow! Thanks for volunteering for chaperone duties!" Cassie just realized that Sam Robbins was walking next to Ellie. Interesting! With her short blonde curls and his handsome dark looks, they were a real-life Barbie and Ken.

Our Mother Away from Home

The theme for the Homecoming Dance was "Under the Sea," one of many themes that Cassie utilized—and repeated--over the years. The Oakview Sheraton was gleaming in nautical décor, which was provided by Nelson Party Planners of nearby Glendale. Professional decorations were part of Cassie's budget for formal dances, giving the ASB students a break.

Sadly, Pete wasn't the Ransom DJ for the Homecoming Dance. Instead, Dave Thomas was the tune-spinner. He was a popular DJ who covered many dances over the years.

As she and Ellie were checking in students, Cassie noticed two senior girls who were overly joyful and giggly. As her instincts quickly kicked in, she ushered them to Marco Cordova and quietly suggested that he breathalyze them. Turned out that the girls had imbibed a pre-dance celebratory beer.

Marco escorted them to an office to call their parents and wait for their arrival to scoop up their daughters. Cassie was happy to hand them over to Marco, who would also follow through with proper punishment after they went before the disciplinary board the next week.

Cassie loved it when Ellie chaperoned, as they enjoyed a running commentary about the students, the hotel staff, and the chaperones. The gig paid $250 for Ellie and the other volunteers, not too bad for four hours of their time.

It was a while before the two had a chance to chat. Did Ellie go out with Sam après-game? Cassie was dying to know. She spotted Ellie looking over the students from one corner of the dance floor, and sauntered over there.

"Oh, Cassie!" Ellie was almost jumping for joy. "Sam and I went for a drink after the game, and it was totally amazing!"

"Do tell!"

"We talked for hours and hours. Kind of like you and Pete."

She continued, "I really, really like him. He is kind and gentle and a hell of a kisser!"

"He's like your very own dark knight! Go for it!"

Cassie liked Sam Robbins, too. She did a walk-through in one of his biology classes, and really admired his hands-on interaction with the students. When she visited, his students were studying the scientific method with experiments involving Sponge Bob Square Pants. It was fun and informative.

The dance was a success! There was just one blink-and-you'll-miss-it moment when freshman princess Sandy Miller's smallish left breast escaped her halter dress, then quickly popped back in. It was while she was dancing to a very upbeat song that the wardrobe malfunction occurred. Cassie happened to be dancing with Tom Reynolds, and she didn't even think that Sandy noticed it. The moment was that fleeting.

Built into Cassie's hotel-dance budget was a room for her at the hosting hotel, so she could chill post-dance and re-charge. She checked in at midnight and contemplated room service which, thankfully, was a 24/7 operation. She hadn't eaten since lunch, and she craved comfort food. She scanned the menu and made her choice: bacon mac and cheese and milk. That sounded great. She ordered and changed into sweats and jumped onto the bed. What a night!

Halloween capped off the month nicely. As is customary at Bennington, the seniors participated in a costume parade around the school, which culminated on the football field, where a photographer awaited their arrival on a scaffold to shoot the senior panorama for the yearbook.

As always, the students' creativity came out to play. There were a few guys who dressed as Jake from State Farm, complete with khakis and red polos. One girl donned a T-shirt with the Bill of Rights emblazoned across it. On her arm was a small stuffed bear attached to elastic. It was her right to bear arms!

The Homecoming King and his girlfriend—Zack and Lexi—displayed their matching Raggedy Ann and Andy costumes.

Getting in on the fun, Cassie dressed as a disco dancer, complete with a mini-dress and go-go boots. She accessorized nicely with love beads and a hair band that matched her dress.

The ASB Officers cast the official votes for the winner of the costume contest--senior Bobby Davidson--who dressed as a photo booth picture strip, with enlarged photos of some of his pals. Cassie never failed to admire the students for their clever display of Halloween imagination.

As she headed home to gather her candy for trick-or-treaters, Cassie felt at peace as the setting sun gave in to a blazing horizon, and the air bit at her cheeks. She bid farewell to Ellie and left Bennington. Little did Cassie know that a special trick-or-treater would be waiting at her door, making this a very special Halloween. All it took was a little collaboration with the top matchmaker in Oakview, who quickly texted Pete upon Cassie's exit.

Damn, I'm good, Ellie declared, patting herself on the back.

Peace out, October.

Chapter Three - November

"I'm pregnant."

Lexi Cassidy's two-word declaration made Cassie jump in her seat. Lexi had quietly closed Cassie's door behind her and slumped into a seat. She looked so broken, so defeated. There were dark circles under her beautiful blue eyes, and her blonde hair had lost its sheen. Before Cassie was not the bubbly cheerleader who inspired students on a Friday night. Instead, there was a lifeless child, desperately in need of guidance and comfort.

Cassie remembered a while back, when Libby Jackson told her that Lexi bolted out of her classroom without saying a word, or asking for permission. It all made sense now: She was plagued with morning sickness.

"Thank you for sharing this news with me, Lexi. I know it can't be easy," Cassie tried to soothe her, despite the severity of the pronouncement.

"Tell me, is Zack the father? I am just assuming he is. Does he know? Do his parents and your parents know?"

"Yes, he is. Our families know.   As of this minute, you are the only person at Bennington who knows."

"Okay, what are your plans? The district asks a pregnant girl to leave campus once she starts showing, which I think is three or four months. How far along are you?"

"I'm three months along, due in May. I plan on placing the baby up for adoption and returning for my senior year. There is an online high school called Options that I am going to enroll in."

Lexi lowered her eyes. "This is my last week at Bennington."

"I have to share this news with Ms. Daniels and the other members of the administration. Mrs. Stone, the registrar, will contact your teachers once you have withdrawn. She will be very discreet. No one needs to know why you are leaving." Cassie tried to be gentle and reassuring.

"I really appreciate your help." Lexi was near tears at this point.   She stood up, took a deep breath, and gathered her thoughts momentarily before bravely voicing them aloud.

"I always think of you as our mother away from home. You always have our backs. I knew that I could come to you and count on you for support."

"Oh, honey!" Cassie leaped out of her chair, rounded her desk, and went in for a big hug, Bruno-style.

"That is one of the sweetest things a student has ever said to me! Let's keep in touch. It is going to be okay."

After Lexi left, Cassie zipped across the hall to Ellie, indicating the need to see the General. Once inside the office, she requested an emergency admin board meeting, ASAP. The General put things in motion, and in 30 minutes all parties were present in the conference room adjacent to her office.

Tom, Christine, Cassie, Marco, and the General sat at the huge table that centered the room. Cassie was the first to speak, as she furtively glanced around the room.

"Constance, thank you for calling this meeting. This afternoon, Lexi Cassidy paid me a visit. It seems that she is three months' pregnant, and this is her final week at Bennington. Zack Peterson is the father."

Cassie had to hand it to her fellow administrators. No mouths dropped open at the revelation. Discretion was one of the predominant principles of Administration 101.

She continued, "I told Lexi that I would give you the news and that Cathy Stone would let her teachers know after she has withdrawn. I think we should have her and Zack be seen by a personal counselor. What do you think?" With that, she glanced at the General.

"Well, Cassandra, I think that is a good idea," the General began. "However, I think that we also need to bring in the couple and their parents to meet with all of us. We all need to be on the same page. Yes, Lexi will be leaving, but Zack will be here until graduation. He needs support as well."

Damn! Gotta hand it to the General, Cassie thought. I guess she deserves to be at the helm of this school.

Christine inquired about Lexi's health, and Tom reiterated the district's stance on pregnancy.

After the meeting, Cassie waved goodbye to Ellie, exhausted after the events of the day. Of course, she couldn't reveal what was happening, even to her BFF, whose face was one big question mark.

Startlingly, Ellie stood up and mimicked a pregnant belly. Yikes! How did she know? Maybe Ellie would be a private investigator in her next job. Cassie raised her hands up in a gesture that said "I can't tell you."

She called it a day by 2:00. And called Pete.

Thankfully, he picked up after two rings.

"Hi, Pete. Are you free to meet me this afternoon? I am done for the day."

"Wow!" Pete was incredulous. "You are never finished with school this early in the day. Yes, I had my nap, and I am free. You just name the place."

He added, "I hope you're okay."

"Yeah, I am okay. I just need to de-stress." *I just need you.* "It has been a difficult day."

"Why don't you meet me at my house? I know you were over last night, but I could really use the company."

"Okay. I am headed right over."

Our Mother Away from Home

Cassie arrived before Pete, and she set out some cheese and crackers and placed a bottle of rosé in a wine cooler. She always kept wine glasses in the freezer so that they were at the ready.

When Pete entered her house, Cassie melted into his arms. All of the stress of the past few hours dissipated as she held on to this wonderful man, who was quickly becoming an integral part of her life.

The two nibbled on the mini-charcuterie board and sipped on glasses of the wine. She realized that she had skipped lunch in the midst of all of the high drama.

"Hey!" Pete was proud of himself for remembering this. "What are you doing for Thanksgiving? My mom wants to invite you for dinner. I know it is a few weeks away, but we would love to have you join us, my brothers, and their families."

"Oh! I would love to join you!"

Usually, Cassie went to Ellie's parents' house. However, Ellie probably had another plus one in mind this year.

"I will come only if I can bring something," Cassie said. "Please let me know what your mom would like."

"Okay, I promise I will ask her. What are your specialties?"

"I love to make bread. Olive bread, focaccia, sourdough. I do a great veggie lasagna, which won't translate well to Thanksgiving. I make three kinds of quiche; again, not appropriate. I also make some dump desserts."

"What are dump desserts?" Pete had to ask.

"They are desserts with just a few ingredients that you just dump into a casserole dish, and bake. I have made cherry, strawberry, you name it. The base is a cake mix."

Pete just laughed. This pixie was always surprising him with her wit and charm. Thanksgiving would be extra special this year.

"I'll ask Mom."

Cassie briefly filled Pete in on her day, without naming names. He just listened and let her recount the events of the past few hours. What a tough job, he thought.

Pete's visit was just the thing to raise Cassie's spirits. They watched a movie and nibbled, and Cassie heated up a frozen veggie pizza. During the second movie, Cassie fell asleep, her head on Pete's shoulder. He slowly got up and gently lowered her to the couch. She woke up when he was kissing her goodbye and threw her arms around his neck, deepening the kiss.

She realized, mid-kiss, that it had been a long time since she had enjoyed kissing a man, especially one as handsome as Pete.

It killed Pete to leave, but he was due at the station by 5:30 in the morning.

"Sweet dreams, lovely pixie." With that, he was off.

Our Mother Away from Home

Cassie did, indeed, have a sweet dream about Pete. She woke up to begin the most beautiful day with the dream on the forefront of her mind. It sustained her through the rollercoaster ride that was her job.

Later in the day, she got a text from Pete.

Mom said she would love to have your homemade bread at Thanksgiving. You choose the kind.

Great! I will surprise you guys!

Cassie ran down her supplies list: flour, kalamata olives, rosemary, and yeast. She would make olive bread and rosemary focaccia.

She loved baking bread. Though it was a time-consuming process, it was a labor of love. She would also make two types of compound butter--herb butter and sundried tomato butter--and bring some regular butter for the kiddos.

As part of the planning of the new Marina Shores High School, the administration met once a month to update everyone on the progress of the school. They had the last two months off, as everyone in the administration was busy with the start of the new school year. Only Dr. Castleberry appeared on the new Marina Shores campus Monday through Friday, along with the construction staff.

The other administrators were Claire Washington, Vice Principal of Academics, and Mike Stevenson, Vice Principal of

Athletics and Technology. Cassie's title would be Vice Principal of Student Affairs/Activities Director.

Cassie loves these meetings, which are held on Saturdays.   Everything that has been completed made the campus seem more and more alive, though the students would not be arriving en masse for ten months. After the meeting, she spends the night at the Pelican Inn, an exclusive bed and breakfast in Marina Shores. The days are long, and she treats herself to a pampering evening, debriefing herself on all of the information that she took in during the day.

The head coaches of the fall sports were hired, and they were in the process of hiring assistants. The gym was finished, as was the performing arts complex, which looked like an off-Broadway theatre.

Cassie's activities center was coming along nicely; she loved that she had a hand in the color palette of the furniture and cabinetry. They mirrored the school colors of blue and green, the colors of the ocean. For the first time, she will have a leadership class, comprised of ASB and Class Officers. No more sex education!

One of these days, she will ask Pete to accompany her on this mini-vacation; he can spend the day at the beach while she meets with her colleagues. Perhaps he surfs.

On November 14, Cassie met with yearbook adviser Tina Caldwell, who sashayed into Cassie's office with her perpetual nose in the air. She wondered if Tina were ever a runway model, in addition to being a hand model.

Our Mother Away from Home

Cassie took the time to peruse the first batch of yearbook pages. She had requested an enlarged shot of the senior panorama, which could possibly be problematic, considering the potential of hand gestures and what not appearing in the photo. Part of the dress code for Halloween was no masks, so Cassie could peruse the faces well.

As she was scanning the photo, Cassie stopped and took a closer look.

"Look here! These four guys are juniors!"

Damn, how did that happen?

"Off to the right side are James Tucker, Billy Moncrief, Andy Carson, and Tony Kelso, looking quite pleased with their stupid stunt."

Tina was flabbergasted.

"I am so sorry, Cassie. I don't know how they slipped into the photo shoot. No one made a ruckus at seeing them. I have to admit that I don't know all of the seniors—or juniors, for that matter--by sight."

Her squared shoulders seemed to deflate, as she scrambled to come up with an answer.

"No one made a ruckus because they were enabling the rascals with their silence. Okay, this is one for Marco," Cassie noted. "Is there any way that you can submit this spread at a later deadline?"

Tina searched nervously for an answer.

"Yes!" Relieved, she went on as a light bulb went off, "We can make these senior candid pages. I have enough pictures to cover them. I will personally finish the pages and run them by you tomorrow morning before Jonathan Bennett picks up the deadline."

She looked to Cassie, "Because the four are to the outside of the photo, it is possible to Photoshop them out. Perhaps as part of their punishment, they will be obligated to pay for the fees that Harvard Yearbooks would charge for the Photoshopping."

Great solution.

Satisfied, Cassie thanked Tina and sent her on her way. She needed a chat with Marco.

ASAP.

Yes, indeed, her job was a rollercoaster ride. One that went at warp speed.

Marco was in the school cafeteria during upper lunch when Cassie spotted him. She called him "Double L," short for Latin lover, which he certainly wasn't!

Married for 30 years, Marco was devoted to his family. But he was a very handsome man, with dark hair and brown eyes that shone when he spotted Cassie.

"Hey, Cass! What's up, Buttercup?"

"Take a look at the senior panorama, Double L. Do you see some junior knuckleheads?"

"Hell, yeah!" Marco blurted out quietly as he scanned the photo, pointing out the four delinquents. "I will plan a disciplinary board meeting for next week and discuss this with Tina."

"Thanks, pal!" Cassie and Marco were not only colleagues, but true friends.

Tina's suggestion for punishment for the Delinquent Four was seconded by the disciplinary board, which asked each student to contribute $50 for Photoshopping and attend two Saturday detentions.

The Monday before Thanksgiving, Patsy returned to the Block Five 20 and clued them in on sexually transmitted diseases. Once again, Cassie slipped out the door, and returned at the end of the period.

And, once again, the class gave a huge thanks to Patsy, who covered the causes and prevention of STDs.

She did a mini-lesson on birth control, as well. She actually had a condom, which mesmerized the class as she waved it around. Nineteen pairs of eyes followed it, as if they were rabid fans at a lively tennis match. Back and forth.

Too bad Declan was absent. He missed out on a memorable lesson that he, no doubt, would find fascinating!

When instruction was over and the two had walked together to the front office, Cassie gave Patsy a Thanksgiving centerpiece, a glass pumpkin with lights inside. It would be perfect for their feast.

"Oh, dear! This is just beautiful!" Cassie had to admit that she purchased a pumpkin for herself, too. "Thank you so much!" Patsy gave her a big hug.

Just as the ladies were exiting the front office, making their way toward the three-wheeled bike, Dr. Castleberry was entering it. He had a lunch meeting with the General. Apparently, they had been friends for years. Guess principals are a close network of professionals.

Cassie introduced the two, who started chatting as if they had known each other all of their lives.

Hmmm, thought Cassie. Two widowed people with grandchildren; one a month away from retirement, one a year and a half away. One tiny little elfin woman, and one stately silver fox.

"Excuse me, but I have a conference call in a few minutes," Cassie hated to interrupt the two, but she had a teleconference planned with Lexi Cassidy's mother. "Thanks again, Patsy! I will see you on Thanksgiving. James, I will see you soon."

"Hey, Cassie, do you mind telling Constance I will be right in?" Dr. Castleberry's idea of *being right in* meant half an hour later, not until he had a nice long talk with Patsy and scored her email address and cell number.

Cassie couldn't wait to do a little gossiping with Ellie.

"Well, Miss Ellie," she told her BFF when they had a moment away from their computers, "I took a page out of your playbook! I introduced Dr. Castleberry to Patsy Patterson, and the rest is going to be history. I think I made a match, right here in the parking lot!" She pointed to where the lot was.

"No way!" Ellie was quick to reply. "That is *my* department! Wow, just wow!"

Over cups of late-afternoon coffee in the break room, the ladies caught up. Ellie had been on three dates with yummy Sam, and she would be accompanying him to his parents' house for Thanksgiving. Cassie called that one! She shared that she, too, had an invitation for turkey day. They would have a lot to talk about on Monday.

"Oh, Cassie!" Ellie knew that she was like a broken record, but she squealed as she said, "I will miss you so much next year!"

That made Cassie's heart hurt. She had done a great deal of soul searching before accepting the Marina Shores job during the previous spring. She understood what Pete had said about a fresh start at KFUNN; that is exactly how she perceived the move to the ocean. But she had a lot of special people she will be leaving behind in Oakview.

Cassie spent Thanksgiving morning literally up to her elbows in flour, as it permeated her skin, hair, and clothes, and sprinkled itself lavishly all over her kitchen island and floor.

Baking bread helped her escape her ordinary world and enter into a fantasy world of being a homemaker, with a few kids and a picket fence and an adoring husband.

She would pick fruit from the trees in the backyard, and bake pies and cobblers. She would be PTA president and soccer mom and Scout volunteer.   That was always the collective dream. It sounded like a cliché, but it was the resounding dream that unrelentingly haunted her for as long as she could remember.

Pete picked her up at 4:00, and they headed over to Patsy's which, coincidentally, was only four blocks from Cassie's house. To think that Pete grew up four blocks away! And she didn't know him!   He now lived in a condo complex a few miles from his mom's place.

Just as Cassie had figured, Patsy's home was warm and welcoming, with copious autumnal decorations making the large home seem more like a cottage.

The glass pumpkin was at the center of the dinner table, and Patsy had added a plaid runner the length of the table. She arranged pumpkins and candles of different sizes. The ambience was Martha Stewart-worthy. Patsy probably has runners and decorations for every holiday.

When they were having pizza a few weeks back, Pete mentioned that Patsy would make a great party planner. I believe it, thought Cassie. The proof was right in front of her, in all of its splendor.

Our Mother Away from Home

Dinner was lively and chaotic. Patrick was with his wife Jackie and their sons Cooper and Riley, 5 and 3 respectively. Parker and his wife Sabrina added to the noise with their sons, Chris, 2, and Drew, 4. Four boys ages 2 to 5, thought Cassie. Yikes!

Patsy, glowing in her autumn dress, loved this mayhem. She admitted that she really wanted a granddaughter one day, but she loved the boys.

No one had a "P" name, Cassie noted. Guess the "P" line stopped with her sons.

Patrick is an English professor at Walker College, where Patsy teaches her labor and delivery nurses-to-be. Jackie is a stay-at-home mom.

Parker works at Oakview First Bank, which meant that he might know if his boss, Harley Keffer, was really in a relationship with Mayor Max. She would find time someday to inquire about it.

Sabrina owns a boutique on Main Street called Main Street Treasures. Cassie thought that Sabrina looked familiar, as she had spent time and money in the darling shop over the years. It really was chock full of treasures.

"So, Cassie," Patrick remarked, "I understand that you are changing jobs next year. I have heard that Marina Shores is going to be just a gem of a school. One of our English teachers serves on the board of education, and he has been updating us on the progress of the school."

"Yes, it is really exciting, Patrick. To be in on the ground floor is fantastic." Cassie explained how much had already been done and what was yet to be completed.

"Please call me Pat," Patrick seemed so sincere, as all of the Pattersons did. What a lovely family!

Just as dessert was being served—pumpkin, apple and cherry pies, with or without ice cream or whipped cream— there was a knock at the door.

Who could that be?

Cassie was stunned when Sabrina opened the door, and there stood Dr. Castleberry! I cannot wait to text Ellie, Cassie thought.

Patsy greeted James, immediately hugging him tightly. The embrace appeared so natural. There was such a connection there, an unexpected and sweet blessing that neither saw coming.

"Everyone, this is Dr. James Castleberry, who is the principal at Cassie's future school, Marina Shores High School. James, these are my children, their spouses, and my grandchildren. And, of course, you know Cassie."

She did a left-to-right sweep of the clan and named them all. The men stepped up to shake hands with James.

Well, well, well! I *did* make a match, thought Cassie. She learned quite well from watching Ellie, the mistress of romance. Ellie would probably be a great romance novelist.

The lively conversation continued, and James just seemed to have quickly woven himself into the fabric of the Patterson family.

He was asked about his own family, Marina Shores, and his retirement, the beacon of hope for his future. Patsy shared that she was so ready for retirement, her days as a labor and delivery nurse and teacher shortly behind her.

Both of them discussed their post-retirement plans.

For James, fishing and babysitting his grandchildren topped the list. Patsy, who earned a Bachelor's degree in journalism, and a Master's degree in nursing, hoped to write for a newspaper, if the opportunity presented itself. She had focused on nursing her whole career, and the thought of writing again held many possibilities.

By 8:00, Patrick and Parker and their families had headed home, and Pete brought Cassie back to her house. James lingered over coffee and pumpkin pie, and parked himself on the loveseat after Parker and Sabrina abandoned it.

Wonder how long he will linger, thought Cassie.

It took two seconds in the car before Pete just had to ask, "Did you know about Mom's supposed new boyfriend?"

"Yes!" Cassie had taken such pride in making the match.

She beamed, "I introduced them! James was coming into Bennington while Patsy and I were exiting when she was my guest speaker on Monday. Boy, they look really tight already."

Taking a different tack as to reassure Pete, she added, "I just adore James. He is a great man. You don't need to worry."

Pete was bewildered.

His mother hardly ever dated, yet she looked so smitten after knowing this guy for only four days. He was a bit skeptical about this match, at first blush.

"Hey, I really liked your bread." Pete decided to change the subject. "Especially the olive bread. You must have been baking all morning."

"Thanks. I loved it. The process is so soothing. It is a great way to spend the day." Cassie really enjoyed baking for others, especially.

"I'm not much of a baker," he said, "but I would love to learn how to make bread."

"I'll be your teacher!" Cassie beamed as she thought of how fun it would be to teach Pete Bread Making 101.

A few minutes later, Pete turned into Cassie's driveway.

"Would you like to come in?" She glanced at him suggestively, eyebrows raised as her eyelids did a little flutter.

"You don't have to ask me twice!" Pete almost bounded out of the car, as eager as a teenager on his first date.

Cassie started a fire, and the pair snuggled on the couch.

"Let's not talk about your mother's love life," Cassie said. "Let's talk about *yours*."

But there wasn't much talking, as Pete lovingly grabbed Cassie's face and kissed her all over, finally landing on her lips. They capped off their Thanksgiving tenderly, each silently whispering thanks for this new love, this cherished, special person.

The Monday after Thanksgiving, the Block Five 20 began its lesson on reproduction. Although Patsy touched on the topic briefly on her first visit, Cassie did a deeper dive into the subject.

At the end of the period, the class was asked to do some investigative thinking before the next time they met: They were to ask their parents where they were born and in what city, at what time, date, and if there were anything extraordinary about their birth.

Cassie thought that this might be a fascinating exercise. Each of them had to present the information to the class next time. Good to get the quiet ones interacting.

She texted Patsy after class.

Our Mother Away from Home

Hey, you'd love this new assignment I just gave my students. They are to get some information on their birth—place, time, circumstance, height and weight. Wonder how many were born with you at their moms' side!

I love it! Let's meet for coffee some Saturday in the future, and you can share their findings.

Would love it! See you soon!

Cassie was excited at the prospect of seeing Patsy again. Just as Pete was making his way into her heart, so was Patsy. Maybe she can get the skinny on the new relationship with James. Hmmm… Her love radar was up!

Ellie popped into Cassie's office mid-morning.

"Wanna do pizza and chardonnay after school? We have a lot to catch up on!"

"Yeeesss! But it has to be around 5:30, as I am going over to Pam Roland's after school. We need to map out next semester. We will miss the cheap pizza, but it should be quiet post-Madness."

"You're on! Let's eat outside so I can bring Dino with me."

Pam Roland was in baby heaven, as little Preston hung lovingly on her hip, cooing and drooling after his snack of carrot baby food. Her house was surprisingly tidy, with all of the baby accoutrements present—playpen, high chair, toys everywhere.

Our Mother Away from Home

A small woman with short dark hair, Pam was the picture of domesticity.

"Cassie, it is so good to see you! I miss all of my Bennington peeps!"

"Look at you, all motherly and beaming! Little Preston is just adorable!"

As if on cue, Preston made his little baby talk, and Pam lit up.

"No wonder you didn't want to come back to school," Cassie said. "I wouldn't either if this precious little boy had come into my life."

Over iced tea and homemade chocolate chip cookies, the ladies discussed the curriculum for the second semester, with some choice gossip sprinkled in. Cassie was certain that the worst of the year was almost over, and she looked forward to teaching health and safety.

"The most important thing about next semester is that you will be in charge of the blood drive in April," said Pam. "The date is on the school's master calendar. I will assist you with the whole process, which includes getting the Red Cross volunteers and others from Oakview General Hospital."

She added, "Also, your students will be dismissed from part of their day to distribute call slips to those who have volunteered to give blood. They can sign up online to do so. On the sign-up sheet, we will list all of the requirements."

Wow, thought Cassie. What an undertaking! Maybe Patsy would be available to help.

Our Mother Away from Home

She left Pam a little after 5:00, and headed to the Pizza Project.

Bruno was his usual jolly self, a kind of year-round Santa Claus. He was actually making pizzas, as Cassie could see from over the front counter. Someone must have called in sick. He gave a robust "Hello!" to Cassie, and waved with a floured hand. It is always so good to see Bruno.

Cassie ordered her wine, and sat at a table outside to wait for Ellie. She glanced at her phone, and saw a text from Pete.

She did a little invisible happy dance all alone at her table. Get a grip, she told herself.

How are you doing today? Sure enjoyed our time together this weekend.

Oh! Me, too!   I am at the PP waiting for Ellie who, apparently, had a steamy weekend with one of our biology teachers. They have been dating since the Homecoming game. Gotta get the deets.

Wow! Doesn't the school district have rules for inter-dating?

No! We have had a few couples who have dated and have even gotten married! Pam Roland, whom I visited today, taught my health class before she decided not to return after giving birth. Her husband Mitch is an art teacher at Bennington.

Well, I have a lot to learn! I will let you go. Please say hi to Ellie!

Will do!

As she approached the table, Ellie seemed to be glowing from within as she clutched Dino.

Things went well with the Robbins clan, a smaller family with two boys, no wives, and no grandchildren. Sam's parents are both doctors at Oakview General; Cassie wondered if Patsy knew them. Of course, she must!

Ellie said that she and Sam decided on an impromptu Vegas trip on Friday and returned on Sunday. They stayed at the Bellagio and watched the magnificent fountains in the evening, arm-in-arm.

She didn't have time to put Dino into a kennel, so she took him with her on the trip, and was so excited that the Bellagio was dog-friendly. Some time ago, along with assistance from her vet, she filed paperwork for Dino to be her emotional support animal. Just in case.

"It was magical, Cassie!" Ellie couldn't help but gush. "Sam is my Prince Charming, my knight in shining armor. I know these are oft-used buzzwords, but is true."

She continued, "I realize this is cheesy, but he should be teaching anatomy, not biology!"

Both ladies dissolved into laughter.

Cassie thought that things were happening quickly between Ellie and Sam, but she didn't comment about it. She and Pete, by contrast, were taking things slowly in the romance department.

Cassie talked about her bread-making, Pete's family, and meeting up with Pam.

"Oh, Ellie! You should see that cute little nugget Preston! He is sooo adorable. Pam is so lucky that she gets to stay at home."

"I would love to go with you next time! I love babies!"

"Okay, let's plan for it."

The lasagna was just excellent, as is everything in Bruno's place. The ladies were stuffed when they exited the restaurant, waving thanks to their good friend. There would be no running for Cassie, who returned home to work on lesson plans for the next day. The Block Five 20 would be making their presentations on their births. Should be a great lesson.

Cassie listened in to Pete the next morning, as she did every morning.

"Hey, all of you in the KFUNN Nation! I want to dedicate this song to a very special person in my life. She knows who she is."

With that, he played "Green-Eyed Lady" from the '70s group, Sugarloaf.

Cassie's breath caught as she listened closely to the lyrics, riveted to the radio. Pete is really speaking to me about my job, she thought. I soothe pain; I solve problems. He really knows me. I know it has been just a few months since we met, but he knows me.

That afternoon, the Block Five 20 shared information about their births.

Most of them had been born at Oakview General, a few had been born at Glendale Hospital, and some were born out of state.

Turned out that Declan and Jody Bridges were born a day apart at Oakview, on January 14 and 15, respectively.

It was a lively exchange of information, as the students were anxious to share their stories, and to learn more and more about their peers.

The largest baby was Tim Kaplan, at 10 pounds, 11 ounces. He kept up his husky profile to this day and was probably the largest kid in the Sophomore Class.

The smallest baby was Sophia Bennington, who weighed in at 5 pounds, 12 ounces. Little did Cassie know that Sophia had a twin brother, Mark, who made an appearance at 5 pounds, 13 ounces. She asked Sophia to bring Mark around to Room 602 one day, so that she could meet him.

Jenny Cooper was a preemie, born three weeks early, and stayed in the NICU until her targeted due date. She weighed in at 6 pounds even.

Cassie simply smiled. It was a great assignment that got the students thinking about their birth and the circumstances surrounding it. She couldn't wait to share her findings with Patsy.

Our Mother Away from Home

November exited as it entered, a warm embrace in the crisp breeze, a comfort like chicken noodle soup in front of a blazing fire.

Life was just fine.

Chapter Four - December

There wasn't much on Cassie's activities agenda for the month of December, as there were only two weeks of school before final exams. Thanks to the ASB students, Bennington was transformed into a winter wonderland, from the offices to the lunch area. Classroom doors looked amazing in advance of the door-decorating contest.

Again, the students' creativity flourished. There were doors based on Christmas songs, such as "We Wish You a Merry Christmas" and "Deck the Halls," classics always utilized in this contest, but they still worked.

In the classrooms, lights adorned the real and artificial trees, and students chose names for Secret Santa gifts.

The Block Five 20 even included Cassie in the name-picking. She chose Porter Sheffield.

Rules for the name-swapping were simple: Spend no more than $5.00 on a homemade present. Cassie knew right away what she would be making: chocolate-covered pretzel rods with red and green sprinkles. Just three ingredients: pretzels, chocolate chips, sprinkles. Definitely more than $5.00, but what the heck!

Our Mother Away from Home

As promised, Cassie kept in touch with Lexi Cassidy, who told her via email that she was feeling better in this, her second trimester.

Apparently, the morning sickness had fallen by the wayside, and in its place were intense cravings for chocolate ice cream and pepperoni pizza.

Lexi sent a selfie with a huge bowl of ice cream, which, when printed, went straight to the wall of love. Fortunately, the photo didn't feature her bump.

The meeting among the administration, Lexi, Zack, and their parents went very well. The plan remained the same: Lexi and Zack would put the baby up for adoption, Zack would go to Stanford, and she would return to Bennington next year after finishing this year at the online school. She would conference with the cheer coach in the summer, to see if there was a spot for her on the squad.

Cassie also kept tabs on Zack, whose prowess on the football field skillfully led his team into the state playoffs, with the regional finals next week. From the outside, he seemed to keep his cool under the stress.

Note to self: Check in with Zack in the post-season.

On the first Saturday in December, Cassie and Patsy met at The Breakfast Nook, a popular Oakview eatery.

Patsy glided into the Nook, resplendent in a Christmas sweater that lit up, but would definitely not qualify in the ugly sweater category.

She was luminous, and it wasn't the sweater. She must have driven her car, as the ubiquitous pink helmet was absent. As is habit, the ladies immediately embraced.

"Oh, Patsy! You look fantastic!"

Cassie also was wearing a Christmas sweater, but it was mild compared to Patsy's yuletide work of art.

"It is always great to see you!" Patsy was grateful for this new, burgeoning friendship.

Notes in hand, Cassie shared her findings about the birth stories of the Block Five 20. Chances are, Patsy could have been the nurse to some of the Oakview babies.

"Wow, 10 pounds, 11 ounces is one big baby," Patsy commented about Tim Kaplan's chubby weigh-in to life.

"Seriously, what is the largest baby that you helped to deliver?" Cassie was curious.

"A little over 12 pounds, and it was a very difficult birth."

Patsy seemed to cringe in remembrance of that challenging day, which involved two doctors and two nurses in a 10-hour labor, and an emergency Cesarean-section birth.

"Luckily, it all went well. I recently ran into Steven and his parents at the hospital, where they visit every year on his birthday, November 30. It is their way of paying homage to everyone involved in his birth. I think it is a lovely thing to do."

Impatient, Cassie could wait no longer. She just had to ask.

"Gosh, Patsy, it was great to see James at your house on Thanksgiving. What a surprise! How are things going with the two of you?"

"Cassie, this is the great love that I never thought would enter into my heart and my life after the death of my dear husband, Scotty. James, as you know, is a terrific man who is devoted to his family. We have so much in common, even though our occupations are vastly different."

Patsy felt so close to Cassie that she was comfortable with admitting her feelings outright:

"I am completely and totally in love!"

Cassie was stunned at the confession, and took a second to wrap her head around it.

"Oh, that is soo great! I am so happy for both of you! Two of my favorite people on Earth, together!"

Crikey, she needed to hold back this information from skeptical Pete. Duly noted.

They were both bouncing up and down in their booth, drawing curious stares from the quizzical breakfast club.

Who cares, thought Cassie. This was a joyful time for the friends, and they gleefully reveled in the moment.

When things settled down, Patsy had a request.

"Hey, Cassie, I wanted to ask you personally if you would come over on Christmas for dinner. Will you come?"

"Of course! Let me know what I can bring."

"Bread, since it was so fabulous at Thanksgiving!"

"Okay! You got it!"

Note to self: Ruminate over the bread possibilities.

Later that evening, Pete came by for dinner so that they could catch up and begin a Christmas-shopping list. They decided to go to the Oakview Mall the next day.

Pete would be purchasing gifts for his mother, nieces and nephews. And, secretly, he would buy something very special for his little pixie, but not tomorrow. Cassie would be gifting Pete, Patsy, Ellie, and (wince) the General. It is just good practice to give your boss a present at Christmas.

"Do you think we're nuts shopping the first week of December?" Pete asked over dinner. The two were sitting side by side, their habit since their post-dance evening in the gym. "I think we should have done this months ago."

"Well, we'll be in good company! Let's plan on going when the mall opens, and the crowds are not as overflowing."

Pete was the impatient one this time, and he didn't hold back.

"I know that you had breakfast with Mom this morning. Did she mention James? I wonder what is up with those two."

"She just said that things are going well." Cassie didn't lie to Pete; she just held back details of Patsy's morning effervescence.

Changing subjects, she said, "Okay, let's plan out our strategy for tomorrow. How about you come get me at 7:30, and we hit up Starbucks before the mall opens? I know it has early shopping hours during the holidays."

They mapped out the stores they would be targeting. With any luck, they would be done by noon. Maybe they'd have lunch at the Pri afterward.

Business out of the way, and the dishes in the dishwasher, they snuggled together on the couch, and the relaxation portion of the evening was under way. Pete took Cassie's face in his hands, and kissed her passionately. Their lips were meant for each other, a perfect, lovely fit.

On Monday, Cassie zipped into the front office and abruptly stopped at Ellie's desk.

"Break room, now!" she demanded.

Ellie's eyes lit up, and she stayed silent until they were both safely alone with the coffee pots.

"Spill!" Her gossip radar was working overtime.
Beep, beep!

Our Mother Away from Home

"I had breakfast with Patsy on Saturday, and she admitted that she was, and I quote, 'completely and totally in love' with James!" She used air quotes for effect.

As if on cue, and without direction, the two started singing "Matchmaker" from *Fiddler on the Roof.*

And started laughing hysterically, tears escaping their eyes.

The friends were movie buffs, and often had sleepover movie nights.

Just then, the General chose to march in for coffee. She cast a disapproving glance at the two, and the laughter halted immediately.

"Ladies, let's get back to work. This is no time for hijinks. We have a lot to do before we leave for winter break on December 20th."

She turned toward Ellie. "Let's go over those employment applications in my office. We have some positions to fill for the second semester."

So much for spontaneous tomfoolery on an early Monday morning in December.

The Jets Football team, now 14-2, successfully made its way into the state final the second week of December, bringing all sorts of emotions in an already-emotional, pre-final chaos.

Our Mother Away from Home

There wouldn't be a rally, which would detract from test review time, but there would be a rooter bus to the game, two hours away at Simcox Academy, an all-boys school. The Jets would be taking on the Concord Cavaliers from Northern California, with Simcox as a neutral site.

Cassie put all of the wheels in motion. She ordered the bus, created the online form for students wishing to take the trip, and asked the ASB's publicity committee to make signs for the venue.

A priority was the final review for the Block Five 20. Cassie decided to have stations around the room, with questions highlighting the curriculum that was covered in the semester. Students were to pair up, and check out the 15 pieces of paper for answers. The first team that got all of the answers correct got mason jars filled with Christmas M and M's.

The game was fun for the 20, and Porter Sheffield was on fire. He loved anything with a game behind it, and was a very competitive person. Cassie had heard that he was an excellent baseball player, a pitcher at that.

Note to self: Attend some sophomore baseball games in the spring.

The stations featured questions about sex and reproduction. Cassie had to admit it: Patsy was right about the fact that the more you talk about sex, the easier it becomes.

Sure enough, Porter and his partner Declan were the victors. The boys high-fived each other, and received their M and M's, the envy of their classmates.

Our Mother Away from Home

During the next class, Cassie played a review Kahoot, an online quiz game that the students played individually. Again, Porter was the clear winner of a McDonald's gift card.

It is nice to see him come out of his shadow, Cassie thought, if only for a while.

Surprisingly, only 25 students purchased tickets for the bus ride to the state championship game—the lowest number that Allied Bus Company would allow, coincidentally.

Cassie accompanied them, along with Christine Walker and the General, who took to walking up and down the aisle, making sure that nothing untoward was happening in the seats. She really was like a general, with her marching and scrutinizing, marching and scrutinizing.

Cassie sat across the aisle from Christine, which gave her some time to get to know her a bit better. This was Christine's second year at Bennington and her first time as an administrator. She is in charge of the faculty and staff, and is the main observer and evaluator, although other members of the administration also observe, especially the new-hires.

"I observed Sam Robbins yesterday," Christine mentioned. "Boy, he is an excellent teacher. He had the students wrapped around his little finger as he was teaching genetics using emojis. It was so creative!"

Just then, one of the students on the bus told Cassie that her friend was having bus-sickness. Christine, a registered nurse before changing careers, grabbed a baggie of crackers and flew up the aisle to tend to the sick one, who was just fine after downing the crackers and water and moving to sit in the very front of the bus for a less bumpy ride.

The students were pumped when the bus stopped at Simcox, and they spilled out to the half-empty stands on both sides of the stadium.

Cassie figured that this was an inopportune time for a football game, with finals next week and Christmas the week after. The game would be televised for those who couldn't attend.

Also, rain was in the forecast for the evening; Cassie was glad that she brought her raincoat and umbrella.

The same sparks were in the air for this game as were present for Homecoming. The marching band, cheerleaders and song leaders had gone on different busses, and were ready to perform at the first state championship in 10 years for Bennington.

Coach Bill Reddick, a Bennie icon and legendary coach of 20 years, marched out onto the field with his team, and the audience roared. Reddick had seen many local and state championships in his celebrated tenure and was Coach of the Year countless times. He was a Bennie alum and went on to play football for the University of Alabama.

Cassie was suddenly stricken at the absence of Lexi as she took to the field and watched the cheerleaders get ready for the game. Next year, for sure.

Our Mother Away from Home

The coin toss dictated that Bennington had the advantage and the ball, and the game commenced. Zack was poised for the challenge, shoulders squared as he took his place in the lineup.

"Let's go Jets!" the Bennington crowd chanted repeatedly, excitement nearly palpable with the rowdy crowd.

Concord was ahead 21-14 at halftime, as Reddick marched off the field with his team, steps deliberate, looking none too pleased. Undoubtedly, he would give the team a harsh dressing down in the clubhouse.

On the field, Cassie scanned the crowd and spotted Marco, who gave her a thumb's up. There was always a huge comfort in that simple gesture, which spoke volumes. Cassie smiled and thumbed Marco back.

In the second half, Bennington was on fire, recharged by Reddick's inspiring but stern speech about the importance of the game and what it meant to the school.

Zack passed for 400 yards and five touchdowns to rally the Jets to a 34-21 victory over the Cavaliers. Cassie couldn't wait to read the newspaper the next day. No doubt, the *Oakview Register* journalist would label Zack a "Stanford commit," a phrase that kept popping up in articles that featured him in recent months.

The passengers filed into the bus, hyped at the victory, chattering loudly.

John Fields, a veteran bus driver for Allied Bus Company, pressed a button and "We Are the Champions" by

Queen blasted through the bus. The Jets screamed and sang along.

An hour into the ride, Cassie chuckled to herself. The kids were asleep! Exhausted from the emotional game, they just conked out. John had already noticed and lowered the volume gradually as more heads nodded.

Christine was out, too. But the General, ever watchful, kept her eyes and ears open as she marched the aisles. No rest for the weary. Or wicked, whichever the case may be.

As the bus pulled into Bennington, rain came pelting down, drenching the Jets as Cassie guided them to shelter under the covered student parking area. One of the rules in riding the bus was that a parent or guardian had to pick up their student after the game.

Surprisingly, the General had nothing but praise for Cassie and Christine.

"Ladies, thank you so much for chaperoning." She seemed sincere. "I thought everything went well."

Is it possible that the General is reverting from a harsh administrator to a kind person? Was the Wicked Witch of Southern California melting, but in a good way?

Cassie was perplexed, once again.

She waited until all of the students had been accounted for, and she dashed for her car in the uncovered faculty parking lot.

Our Mother Away from Home

It was nearing midnight as she pulled into her driveway, exhausted and drenched, but so happy for the Jets' victory.

She texted Bill Reddick her congratulations.

Monday was the beginning of finals week, and the Jets were subdued and studious, the opposite of their game demeanor. Signs appeared in the lunch areas and library, asking for silence in compliance with "Quiet Week."

The Block Five 20 was prepped for its 100-question final, confident and ready to begin as Cassie gave directions.

After the test, everyone exchanged gifts. Cassie received two movie tickets, popcorn, and chocolate candy from January, who seemed so pleased at her proffered gift. Porter was happy with his chocolate-covered pretzel rods. A chorus of "Merry Christmas" resounded through Room 602 when the bell rang, noisily ushering the students off to their next exam.

As Cassie scanned their finals, she kept peeking at the scores, which ended up being outstanding. No one got lower than a B in the class, which pleased her beyond measure.

The quiet at Bennington gave the teachers the opportunity to focus on tests and grades.

The door-decorating judging was done on the sly by the ASB Officers, who declared the front office the victor, with a "Let it Snow" theme.

Our Mother Away from Home

Ellie must have been behind the decorations, which featured snow from a blower, trees and even a snowman. All of the staff who worked in the office would be getting a free lunch from Pizza Project in January. Cassie requested that Bruno, once again, come by to say hello.

She loved him like a second father, something that she was realizing more and more as time went on. It is funny how, initially, Bruno was closer to Ellie because of her work experience at the Project, but that closeness seemed to have transferred to Cassie as well.

On Wednesday, Cassie and Pete and Ellie and Sam had an early double date, eating at the China Place before the annual Christmas tree lighting in the town square. There was a comfortable conversation among the four, who meshed well.

All agreed that they were in the entertainment business—Pete on the air, Ellie in the front office, and the teachers in front of the class.

"A good teacher, like a good entertainer, first must hold his audience's attention, then he can teach his lesson." Cassie found this quote on her phone, from John Henrik Clarke, an African-American historian and professor. It was perfect. She shared it with the table.

With pina coladas and mai tais in hand, the friends toasted Ellie, who had finished her Bachelor's degree online that week. The plan was for her to remain at Bennington until the end of the year, so that she could be with Cassie before she moved on to Marina Shores. Then, she would seek a job in the business field.

"To Ellie," bellowed Sam, "An amazing woman and, now, a college graduate. The best of luck to you, honey!" With that, he leaned over and kissed her.

The beauty of the tree in the town square reminded Cassie of the Christmas scenes in Hallmark movies, where every town was a village bathed in Christmas splendor.

Mayor Max was on hand to do the tree-lighting honors. He truly loved his job as mayor, which was a sharp contrast to his equally important job as an attorney. He beamed to his constituents and gleefully counted down to the big reveal.

"Three, two, one! Merry Christmas, Oakview!!!!"

Everyone ooh'ed and ahh'ed and the tree shone brightly with hundreds of lights and bulbs, decorated by Oakview's fire and police departments, a longstanding tradition.

In the crowd behind Max, Harley Keffer was beaming as well. He wore a red sweater and green scarf, and Max had the opposite. They both resembled town elves.

Hmmm... Maybe Cassie didn't need to chat with Parker about this relationship. Or, maybe she did!

The next day, Cassie perused Zack Anderson's schedule and called him in during the block when he is an aide in the Counseling Office.

"Hey, Miss Greenwood!" he called out at Cassie's open door.

"Hi, Zack! Would you mind closing the door as you come in?"

He looked terrific, thought Cassie.

"How are you doing?" Cassie was hoping he felt as good as he looked.

"I'm great. Stoked about Stanford, and about our championship."

"It was a wonderful game, Zack. Have you heard from Lexi lately?"

"We talk daily, and I try to stop by once a week, at least. She misses Bennington and all of her friends."

He added, "We have been interviewing potential parents for our baby."

Oh, wow.

"How has that been going?" Cassie had a flash of her own, imagining her parents doing the same 32 years ago.

"Along with both sets of parents, we have been meeting with someone from the adoption agency, which vets the couples—or, in some cases, single parents—before we meet them. It is down to two couples, one straight and one gay."

Our Mother Away from Home

When she said goodbye to Zack, she wished him luck and a merry Christmas. She would be emailing Lexi before the end of the week.

They are so young to be making such a monumental decision, one that would affect the rest of their lives. But Cassie had faith in these young people, mature beyond their years.

She was surprised when she received a text from James at the end of that week. Seems that the big grey elf was planning a surprise retirement party for Patsy on Christmas Day, and he needed her help.

He didn't have any contact information for Patsy's kids, and he wanted to consign jobs to them. Cassie texted Pete to enlist his help.

Hi! Are you available for dinner at my place tonight?

Heck, yeah! What is up?

James has transformed himself into a big elf. Will explain. Can you come by at 6?

I will be there! Do you need anything?

Just a partner in crime.

I can do that!

Over chile-cheese quiche and (unfortunately, not homemade) sourdough bread, Cassie filled Pete in on James's secret plan. She got phone numbers of his brothers and sisters-in-law to pass to James, and, secretly, added them to her own phone, in case she would need them in the future. She hoped that she would.

As the week progressed, James had delegated all of his jobs.

Decorations, check. Patrick and Jackie will provide balloons and streamers, and any signs they could create.

Retirement tiara and sash, check. Parker and Sabrina were all over those.

Plane tickets for two to Maui, paid half by all of the kids and half by James, check. Pete and Cassie purchased these, with an open-ended date. The vacation would be dictated by James's schedule, but, hopefully, it would be soon.

Maui was Patsy's favorite place on earth, as she honeymooned there with Scotty and spread his ashes there when he passed away, her entire family by her side.

On the last day of school before their three-week vacation, the students were dismissed at noon after their last exam, and the faculty and staff enjoyed a luncheon catered by the Oakview kitchen staff.

Cassie emceed the festivities, which included an ugly-sweater contest. She and the faculty moderators of each class declared Neil Williams, Pam Roland's replacement, the contest winner. His sweater featured Mr. and Mrs. Claus fully clothed in a hot tub, the reindeers peering skeptically from the sidelines. Blinking lights covered the entire

sweater. Neil's white beard only added to the ensemble, making him appear Santa-like.

With school out of the way, Cassie focused on finishing her shopping, but she also decided to drop by KFUNN the next week, to see where Pete spent his mornings.

She slept in on Monday morning and secretly appeared at the station by 9:30, much to the surprise of Pete, who welcomed her into his weekday digs. She handed him a basket of blueberry muffins, another great surprise.

Stuffed panda bears were everywhere—on shelves and tables and hanging from the ceiling. Pete had mentioned on one of their dates that he receives them as gifts from listeners, and, twice a year, donates them to Children's Hospital of Oakview (CHOO).

"I know that you probably don't have visitors when you are on-air, but this was a rare opportunity, being away from school on a weekday. I thought that I would check out your workplace."

"This is the absolute best surprise!" Pete's day was made with his pixie's unexpected visit. He grabbed her for a quick hug and kiss.   His station manager, Bob Crosby, stared in amazement, all bug-eyed. Pete introduced Cassie and Bob to one another.

"Make yourself at home," said Pete. "The coffee is really bad, but I am hoping that the company makes up for it."

Cassie watched in astonishment as Pete deftly handled the controls, plugging in commercials between songs and maintaining a friendly one-sided conversation with his audience. Callers did weigh in when he hosted his two-minute trivia contest, and the winner won a KFUNN mug with pictures of all of the DJ team. She wanted to snag one of those!

The question: Who wrote the Christmas classic, "Jingle Bells"?

The answer: James Pierpont

Fun fact: "Jingle Bells" was initially published under the title "One Horse Open Sleigh"

Taking a break between Christmas songs, Pete decided to once again devote a song to Cassie.

"KFUNN Nation! This next song goes out a special visitor who brought me muffins this morning. We don't usually play '60s songs, so don't tell the station manager!"

With that, he played "You've Made Me So Very Happy," by Blood, Sweat, and Tears.

Off-mic, Pete sang along with the lyrics, his eyes focused on Cassie.

She never felt more in love than at this moment, a realization that had been tapping at her heart for months. She was in love. Pure and simple.

Our Mother Away from Home

Christmas morning found Cassie back to bread making. On the menu today: brioche, biscuits, and cornbread. Her compound butters would be garlic chive and maple bacon.

While she was kneading the biscuits, she reflected on what she called Christmas magic, those wonderful, unexpected things that happened around the holidays.

There was the Christmas after her high school break-up, when her parents whisked her off to Lake Tahoe--on the border of California and Nevada--where Cassie learned how to ski. And the Christmas when she was eight years old, and a puppy lay in a basket under the tree. And last year, when one student gave her an Oakview Mall gift card worth $100.

It seemed that every Christmas had its own magic, and it came in myriad ways.

Pete arrived at 3:00, and took in the aromas wafting through the house. He grabbed Cassie, twirled her around, and wished her a merry Christmas.

They exchanged gifts: Pete gave Cassie a necklace with a beautifully detailed panda bear charm. She gave him a bread maker, practical but something he would really like.

Christmas dinner was as chaotic and wonderful as Thanksgiving.

Patsy's home smelled of cinnamon and cloves, which Cassie surmised must have its origins with a concoction simmering on the stove. Her Christmas tree was luminous, with bulbs and lights only in red and gold. Wide gold ribbon cascaded down the sides of the tree, and a large gold angel sat atop it.

It was all so breathtaking, Cassie feared that she might cry. Suddenly, she was filled with emotion, watching this wonderful family interact, and wanting so badly to be part of it.

Patsy was touched when the retirement decorations were strewn around the house and set up by her whole family. Though they clashed with the Christmas décor, they were welcomed nonetheless. She donned her tiara and sash.

James arrived for dessert, and he gave a little speech before revealing the big gift:

"Patsy, your family and I are very proud of you, and we celebrate you today. Congratulations on a successful career, one in which you lovingly cared for your patients and helped bring many lucky babies into this world. You deserve the time to care for yourself, to do whatever you wish. I look forward to being alongside you when I, too, retire."

With that, he kissed Patsy, and gave her the tickets.

"Oh, James! This is so wonderful!"

"The gift is from everyone in the room, and there is no date, as the tickets are open-ended. We will go to Maui when our schedules click."

Patsy hugged everyone, tears filling her cheeks as she was overcome with love in abundance. How lucky she is to have so much love in her life.

Pete and Cassie were both quiet on the short drive to her house. It was if they both anticipated what was to follow.

Wordlessly, Cassie took Pete's hand in hers and led him to her bedroom. Gently, he lowered her to the bed and rained kisses upon her face, neck, and chest. Deftly, he unzipped her beautiful green Christmas dress, which accentuated her eyes, and commenced kissing her breasts and stomach. She shivered in reply, feeling alive for the first time in many, many years.

She reached for Pete's shirt, and, slowly for effect, unfastened the buttons, one at a time. He audibly moaned with each button. She did the same with his jeans, which took forever to slip down his legs.

A modern woman, Cassie supplied a box of condoms from her bedside table and passed one to Pete.

It was as if the wait for intimacy was meant to be, as intense as it was. Sensations were heightened, and the couple could not stop from touching each other. They explored the other's body, as if finding buried treasure that came to life.

Later, spent but invigorated by the lovemaking, the pair lay side by side, arms entwined.

Inspired by the moment, Pete gently kissed Cassie and whispered, "I love you." She simply smiled and said, "I love you, too."

That was her Christmas magic.

Chapter Five - January

Still relishing the memory of her lovely intimacy with Pete, Cassie was brought quickly back to reality on the first day back from Christmas vacation.

"Miss Greenwood, Miss Greenwood!"

"I saw you at the Christmas tree lighting in the town square with that Panda DJ guy from the bus benches," Declan declared, standing up next to his desk, hands on hips to emphasize his very important announcement before class started.

Happy New Year to you, too, thought Cassie.

"Is he your boyfriend?"

Oh, the joys of living in a small town. She had no other choice but to tell the truth.

"Yes, Declan, he is my boyfriend." A hush fell over the classroom.

Ignited by the news, Declan burst into applause, and his classmates rallied and did the same.

Our Mother Away from Home

"Yeah, Miss Greenwood!" he declared, as if he were giving the stamp of approval on the couple's union.

This boy needs a life, thought Cassie.

The class began its first chapter on health, which focused on wellness of mind and body. Cassie had no problem with the subject matter and said a prayer of thanks for the new semester.

Today, she talked about nutrition and the five food groups: grains, vegetables, fruits, meat and other protein, and dairy.

The assignment for the Block Five 20 was to bring in a favorite family recipe, with the food groups labeled next to the ingredients.

When class was over, she slipped into the front office and visited her BFF.

"How was your vacation?"

"Christmas was at my parents' house, but we spent Christmas Eve with the Robbins clan. It was a wonderful celebration all around. Sam suggested that we take a small vacation, so we went up to Big Bear Lake for the New Year. We snowboarded and sat by the fire and just enjoyed each other's company. It was the most relaxing vacation." Ellie smiled brightly at the sweet memories.

Cassie shared the touching story of Christmas and the big elf's surprise, but she didn't share about the intimacy between her and Pete. It was too personal, too soon. However, she did mention how they stayed up for New Year's

105

Eve, as Pete didn't have to work the next day, as it was a Sunday.

They decided to abandon their men on Friday for a girls' night in/sleepover at Cassie's, movies to be determined. It was important that they carved time for each other, especially in light of Cassie's impending move. But they didn't like talking about that.

Tina Caldwell came in later that week, with a new batch of yearbook pages ready for the January 15 deadline. As usual, she was noses up as she entered Cassie's office. Somehow, that gesture made her seem taller than her 6-foot stature.

The pages highlighted fall sports, clubs, and candid photos from the Welcome (Back) Dance and Homecoming Dance. The senior panorama had been touched up by Albert Jones Photographers, the Delinquent Four deleted.

"These pages look great," Cassie remarked as she skimmed the photos and took the time to read the copy.

Tina had really utilized her graphic artist background in the designs of the pages. The theme of the book was "A Surprise in Every Direction." It explored behind-the-scenes fun facts that not every Jet knew about Bennington.

For example, the campus was initially a dairy farm in the 1950s and was defunct by the time the Bennington family bought the property. And, in the little theatre, there is a framed photo of Bennington's drama coach, Victor Cruz, standing alongside Jo Jo Cruz, his actor-brother who is famous for his starring role in the soap opera *The Very Best of Us*.

Tina used directions and signs—such as Stop and Slow Ahead—in clever ways throughout the book. And the students had done a wonderful job on the articles and photos so far.

The next weekend the Marina Shores group gathered to share new information. As usual, Cassie checked into the Pelican Inn for the weekend, as being so far from Oakview ruled out a commute home each night. And, because she had a special guest.

James gave a report on the progress of the buildings: the science, English, visual arts, and foreign language buildings were complete. What remained was the math building.

The sports fields were coming along nicely and would be finished in a month's time.

Cassie shared that she used her networking skills in arranging for Albert Jones Photographers to shoot the students' mug shots and the Welcome Dance. Both dates she added to the master calendar.

She was in the process of signing contracts with local hotels for Homecoming, the Sweetheart Dance, and Prom. One small thing that was not cemented yet was which classes would be allowed to attend the formal dances. Were freshmen allowed? Sophomores?

James advised Cassie that the issue would be on the February agenda and asked the core faculty group to think about it until then.

As one of his first duties as principal, James had already hired a photographer/videographer to come in weekly to document the school's progress since the first buildings had begun construction. The video spots would be compiled into a movie to be shared with the board of directors before the general public. It would be a great PR tool.

Claire Washington passed along information about calendar dates for SAT and ACT testing, with Marina Shores as a test center. Also, she listed the teachers who would be taking on AP classes in such subjects as AP Computer Science, AP Statistics, AP Spanish Language, and AP English Literature.

Mike Stevenson said that all coaches and assistant coaches had been hired, and he set up dates for mandatory CPR classes for all coaches, beginning in May. He coordinated these dates with the Oakview Fire Department, whose members would double as teachers for the event.

His next task was to set up summer camps for all sports.

Pete came along for the weekend and he busied himself with reading a novel and checking his schedule for the month. He relaxed and called his mother and brothers, catching up on all of his family while he had the chance.

He ordered room service for lunch, a chicken wrap and French fries—always with barbecue sauce on the side. He was glad that the hotel had barbecue sauce, as not every restaurant carried it.

As Cassie learned early in their relationship, Pete is a very, very picky eater. No ketchup, mustard, or mayonnaise. No ranch dressing or guacamole. Avocados, yuck!

It wasn't as if these items were absent from his family's fridge; he just had an aversion to the creamy stuff.

He was the brunt of his brothers' incessant jokes over the years, which he accepted begrudgingly. They called him Mr. No Condiments, which morphed into Mr. No Condoms when he was a single guy.

One girlfriend actually broke up with him because of his peculiar eating habits. She was tired of his taking so long to order a meal in a restaurant.

Pete just hoped that Cassie would accept him, warts and all, because he intended to be in her life forever.

Cassie returned to the Pelican Inn at 5:00 that afternoon and joined Pete in their in-room hot tub, languishing in the warmth, the stress of the day forgotten. She would make notes on Sunday in the big binder that contains copious Marina Shores notes. It is a chronological listing of the admin meetings since they began the previous summer, with Cassie's annotations throughout.

Our Mother Away from Home

The couple decided to have supper in the dining room, a cozy spot with a large fireplace in the middle of the room, and booths instead of tables and chairs.

Cassie had never enjoyed the B & B as much as this. She usually just crashed after the meetings, but now she had a reason to be up and about, and it felt good.

The place was empty, and the waiter chose a booth right across from the fireplace. It was perfectly romantic. She and Pete had a leisurely meal and shared a bottle of wine, as no driving was in the offing tonight. It was just the relaxation that they both needed.

Pete dropped Cassie off at her house at noon on Sunday, and she readied herself for the week, creating lesson plans and cleaning her house. She was excited to learn what recipes the Block Five 20 would be bringing in on Tuesday, when she saw them next. Maybe she would even have them vote on a favorite, and then make it for the students.

The General greeted her early on Monday morning, asking for a meeting ASAP.

"Is now okay?" Cassie always hitched a breath and braced for what was to come when the General came calling. Everything was ASAP with her.

"Come on in." The General led her into her office, marching to her place behind the desk.

Our Mother Away from Home

"As you know, Cassandra, the search committee has been interviewing for your replacement for the past few months. It has come down to two people, both of whom have had impressive experience in administration. We would like you to meet with them and get your opinion."

"No problem," said Cassie. She had been miffed when she discovered that she was not invited to be included in the search committee, but she was curious to know who was selected.

"Good. You can get their contact information from Ellie."

Cassie waited until Ellie was off the phone to approach her.

"Hey! Do you have any intel on my potential replacements?"

Ellie beamed. "You would not believe it, but one of the candidates was a Vice Principal at Sam's former school! His name is Ronny Goldwyn. Apparently, the school, which is private, is having budgetary problems, and may be shut down. I think Sam dodged a huge bullet there."

She continued, "The other candidate, Katie Francis, just moved from San Francisco. Her husband, a Technical Sergeant in the Air Force, was transferred to Oakview to begin his Master's degree at Walker College. He will be a teacher on the base in Glendale, as well."

"What do you think?" Cassie wondered who her successor might be.

"I think they are both great candidates. Of course, they could never fill your shoes, but they seem like capable people."

Cassie felt strange, thinking about leaving Bennington after 10 years, and meeting her replacement. She emailed both of them and made appointments to see both on Friday, as she had no class that day.

On Tuesday, the Block Five 20 all came ready to introduce their dishes, all marked up with the food groups.

January Propst chose spaghetti and meatballs, one of her mother's favorites, as she was born and raised in a huge Italian family.

"Okay," she began, "We have ground beef and Italian sausage, of the meat group. Eggs in the dairy group. Spaghetti sauce is made from spices, tomatoes, onions, and green peppers, the veggie group. And the noodles are wheat, and in the grain group." Pleased, she shot Cassie a 100-watt smile.

"Excellent!" Cassie was pleased that the students embraced this project.

She heard from Sophia Bennington (fried chicken), Declan McIntosh (corned beef and cabbage), and Jenny Cooper (chicken noodle soup).

Recipes were passed around, and the class favorite was the spaghetti and meatballs, by far.

Note to self: Copy the recipe to make for the class before the end of the semester.

Cassie continued the nutrition discussion for the rest of the class period.

Later that day, Pete texted:

Hey, what's up?

Hi there! Had a great class today! On another note, the General wants me to meet with my potential replacements, to give my assessment of their readiness for the job.

Wow! That's great! I know you were miffed that you couldn't be in on the search team.

Yeah. Sure was. Am meeting with them separately on Friday. How are you doing?

Want to meet after school for pizza? I am starving. Didn't have lunch because we were on location at the Oakview Mall, shooting the Old Navy grand opening.

Yes! See you about 5:30.

Cassie purposefully arrived at the Pizza Project before the designated meeting time, to indulge in a Bruno-hug and chat with him.

"Cassie! *Cara*! How are you doing, Love?"

"Wonderful! How are you?"

"Just great! I have magnificent news! Our daughter, Gianna, is going to have another *bambino*! That will be number 11!"

Bruno's smile was infectious, as he grinned from ear to ear. Cassie went in for another hug.

"That great! I have never been to your house, but it must be huge to accommodate your growing family!"

"Oh, it is! Maria and I must have you and Pete over sometime."

"I would love that!"

Pete arrived, and Cassie did her little memorization thing. This time, she noted how his eyebrows arched way up high when he smiled. And his arm felt warm and safe around her shoulder.

The winter sports were in full swing, and the Bennington administration divvied up duties, between basketball, soccer, and wrestling, covering the home games/matches.

On Thursday, Cassie had double duty: boys' and girls' basketball games. She stayed at school until the girls' game at 6:00, perusing Ronny Goldwyn's and Katie Francis's resumes and cover letters in advance of her meetings the next day.

Ronny had chalked up five years as an administrator, all at Rogers Academy, an all-girls private high school in nearby Lexington. Previously, he had taught history at Glendale High School for six years.

Katie was a stay-at-home mother before she went back into the classroom seven years ago, teaching biology before becoming an Assistant Principal the past three years at Portnoy High School in San Francisco.

Both Ronny and Katie were activities directors at their former schools. And they both looked terrific on paper.

It was close to 11:00 when Cassie returned home. She texted Ellie:

Hey, I am going to come to school at about 9:00 tomorrow. Just got home from the games. Exhausted! Gonna rest up for my interviews tomorrow.

On Friday, Cassie met with Ronny and Katie, at 10:00 and 11:00, respectively. She was blown away by both of them, and seriously could not recommend one over the other, if given the responsibility of choosing.

She tried to think of some difficult questions. For example, she asked what the mission statement of Bennington was comprised of. What was the school mascot? How did the school get its name? What is the current population?

Damn, both did their homework. And, damn, it was a total toss-up.

As Cassie escorted Katie out of the front office, she concluded that she needed to see the General ASAP. Ellie ushered her in to her boss's office.

"Thank you, Constance. In the interest of full disclosure, I have to say that both Ronny and Katie were both great candidates. I was impressed by their resumes and their research regarding Bennington."

"Cassandra, I appreciate the input. I will share your assessment with the members of the search committee." Constance stood, tantamount to saying "This meeting is concluded," and led Cassie to the door.

Don't let it hit you on the way out, Cassie thought.

In the mood for a friendly, lighthearted conversation, she headed to the student cafeteria in search of Marco. He was such a positive force in her life. He would never know how many times his very presence cheered her up. Unless it was regarding a discipline issue.

"Buttercup!" He, too, was delighted to see his friend.

"How ya doing, Double L?"

"Just fine presently, but we have a disciplinary board meeting coming up," Marco said. "Our druggy dogs found some pot in a few lockers."

"Yikes!" Cassie was not part of the disciplinary board; Tom Reynolds and Constance were the other administrative representatives, in addition to Marco.

Our Mother Away from Home

"Yup. Two sophomore boys. Brett Boyd and Porter Sheffield."

Cassie let out a small, but pronounced, yelp. It caused some students to pause mid-sandwich.

"Oh my gosh, Marco! Porter is one of my students!"

"Okay, I can tell you this much. As one of his teachers, you will be asked to write a character reference before we have the meeting with the board and his parents. Look for an email regarding it by the end of the day."

Cassie was bewildered. That skinny little boy, a pothead?

"Thanks, Marco. Good luck with this one."

She was sorely in need of some serious Pete time. She texted him:

Hi there! How is it going?

Great! How was your day?

A tad on the stressful side. Feel like grabbing a bite out? I am too tired to cook.

Sure! Primavera? We haven't been there in a while.

Great! And plan on a sleepover. Bring some clothes for tomorrow.

Sounds great! Will do!

Gina Toledo, adorned in her requisite Italian flag apron and always directing traffic and in constant motion, greeted the two, and ushered them to a quiet table. She knows couples, thought Cassie. Probably has seated them thousands of times.

As she glanced at the menu and saw spaghetti and meatballs, she gleefully recounted the success of the recipe assignment.

And, thoughts of the Block Five 20 led her to Porter Sheffield.

"I learned something today about one of my students," she said, "and it broke my heart."

She recounted what Marco had told her, and talked about Porter, probably a 95-pound pitcher and, apparently, star of the Boys' Sophomore Baseball team.

"Hey, I just met a new sports reporter for the *Oakview Register*, whose last name is Sheffield. Frank Sheffield. Seems like a really nice guy. The paper is on the second floor of our building, and KFUNN is on the first floor, as you know. He mentioned that his kid Porter goes to Bennington, and plays baseball. Bet he's the one."

"I can't divulge Porter's last name, even to you. However, I can share that I have had some concerns about him since the beginning of the year, as sometimes he is really quiet, and, when we play games, he is on fire and just loves them. I think I need to have a personal counselor see him, especially in light of recent developments."

That said, Cassie put all thoughts of Bennington and Porter aside, and enjoyed her time with Pete.

I don't want anything to ruin this precious time, she thought.

The next day, Cassie emailed Lexi Cassidy, and inquired about the pregnancy. Lexi responded right away.

Ever hear of the phrase fat and sassy? That is me! I gained 25 pounds over the course of my pregnancy, and I am feeling really well. Can you believe that I am approaching my third trimester? It doesn't seem possible. I heard that Zack told you about the couples that we interviewed. I think that we are leaning towards the gay couple. I have to say that the thought of separation from my baby hasn't hit me yet. It probably will as I get closer to the birth in May.

Cassie's reply was not only informative for Lexi but left Lexi feeling happy to have received such a warm, caring note from a teacher.

What a huge decision to make at such a young age. I want you to know that I inquired about personal counseling at Options. Even though it is an online school, you have full access to academic and personal counselors. Also, since you have re-registered for Bennington, you may make use of our counseling services. Please think about it. I am so glad to hear that you are feeling well. Take care, Lexi. I will be in touch. Contact me if you need anything.

At mid-afternoon, Cassie felt the need for coffee and conversation with Ellie. She found her BFF at her desk and waited until she was off the phone.

"Coffee break?" asked Cassie.

"You bet!" Ellie had been organizing a meeting for the search committee, and needed a break.

"So, how is everything?" Cassie asked.

"Just working on getting your replacement solidified. The General is setting up a meeting of the search committee, to nail down the choice. You know how she is. Everything is ASAP, chop-chop, get the job done."

Suddenly, Cassie was taken aback. She was aware of the decision that she made last summer, but the reality was hitting her between the eyes that her replacement would be hired imminently, and her focus would soon be solely on Marina Shores.

"What is happening this weekend?" Ellie seemed to sense when her friend was tense, and changed the subject. She would make a great psychiatrist, for sure.

"Just a boys' soccer game Friday afternoon."

"Well, I think we should have a double date on Saturday. And, I have a proposal: What do you think of going away with our guys during Presidents' Day weekend next month? You have the Sweetheart Dance the weekend before, but there are no activities on the calendar for that weekend."

"Wow! You sure did your homework, Ellie! I think your plan is just terrific! We can all get to know each other better. Let's do it!"

Cassie was buoyed by Ellie's suggestion, as she pondered destinations on her way back to her office.   San

Diego? Temecula? Santa Barbara? Perhaps Las Vegas, or Laughlin. She was excited about a little vacay, which, she was sure, both couples would heartily welcome.

Just as she was wrapped up in her revelry, fantasizing about poolside mai tais, the General marched into her office. Cassie was quickly transported back to reality. Miss ASAP is here!

"So, Cassandra," the General began, "I heard that one of your students got caught in Marco's pot bust." Her tone was accusatory, as if Cassie herself had willingly and enjoyably toked with the kid.

"Yes, that's correct. Porter Sheffield is my student, and I sent Marco my character reference the same day that he sent it to me."

"Did you see any warning signs that might have alerted you to this behavior?"

"No, none. I did refer him to personal counseling because he has had repeated mood swings over the course of the year. He has high highs, and low lows. If he is not participating in a game or a competition in class, he is closed off and keeps to himself. I cannot figure him out."

"What did Rachel Singleton offer as a report?" The General was referring to the personal counselor.

"Because of counselor-patient confidentiality, I only got a vague report. Dr. Singleton seemed to think that Porter is just a regular hormonal teenager with mood swings like any other 15-year-old boy."

Cassie was, quite frankly, disappointed with the prognosis, and hoped that Rachel would keep in touch with Porter, and gave more reports, however vague they may be. It was out of her hands.

"Oh, I see," replied the General. "Thank you. Just remember: All of us who work with students are mandated reporters. If you see something untoward, and feel that a child is in danger, you must report it to Rachel Singleton and Child Protective Services."

With that, she marched out of Cassie's office. And that was that. Lecture number 506, concluded.

Later that afternoon, Cassie had class with the Block Five 20. They continued their discussion of nutrition and the importance of incorporating all of the food groups in their daily meals.

"How many of you skip breakfast?" Cassie asked.

About half of them raised their hands.

"How many of you have a coffee drink instead of breakfast?"

Again, about half.

"Well, I'm not surprised. I know that we all have busy lives, but I urge you to consider eating breakfast. There are so many possibilities for on-the-go meals, even some that you can make ahead and freeze. Think about an egg sandwich on an English muffin. And there are several recipes for overnight oatmeal which are delicious. I think

that next time we will look at some possible breakfast recipes that I want you all to make."

Note to self: Peruse easy breakfast recipes.

The double date at Oakview Bowling Alley was a blast for the two couples. Ellie and Sam schooled Cassie and Pete, winning two games out of three. Sam even had a turkey—three strikes in a row. Seems that he has been a lifelong bowler and has won many awards over the years.

"You're a ringer, dude!" complained Pete. "Totally not fair!"

Everyone laughed at the accusation.

"Hey, no one asked me if I had any bowling experience!" shot back Sam.

Ellie was anxious to chat about their impending mini-vacay.

"Okay, I say that we hold a vote about Presidents' weekend. We have talked about San Diego, Temecula, somewhere at the ocean, Las Vegas, and Laughlin. What are your thoughts?"

"I think that, since we only have a few days, we should find some place closer to Oakview," Cassie chimed in.

"Good idea, babe." Pete seconded the thought.

"Okay, that leaves San Diego, Temecula, and the ocean. Let's vote," said Ellie, who always seems to take charge. But that was fine with the others.

"I vote Temecula," said Pete.

"I vote San Diego," Cassie always loved her time there. "Plus, that takes up two of the possibilities, as San Diego is at the ocean."

"Good point, Cassie," said Sam. "But my vote is for Temecula."

That led to Ellie's vote.

"Oh, the pressure!" she said. "Okay, I third the vote for Temecula, with the promise of San Diego in our futures. Just think! If we stay at one of the wineries, we can have a tour and do some spa things! And, if we aren't too squeamish, there are hot-air balloon rides. Plus, there is a casino in town. Good times ahead, people! Good times!!!"

"I don't know about the hot-air balloon rides," Cassie shuddered. "I have a fear of heights, you guys."

"Don't worry about it," Pete assured. We'll cross that bridge when we get to it."

Ellie volunteered to look into the wineries and texted out her report by the end of the next day.

They all agreed on West Temecula Winery, which was a wedding venue as well. They locked in dates, and everything was set in motion.

Cassie got a text from Patsy later that day:

How are you doing, dear?

Just great! How about you?

James and I are having the time of our lives! That is, in between his endless meetings with construction people, city planners, district folks, etc. What an undertaking for a 70-year-old man! But he is really enjoying the creation of this new endeavor and placing his stamp on every facet of it.

Hey, when are you having your next meeting with the Marina Shores administration? Will Pete be accompanying you?

In two weeks—we are meeting bimonthly now. Yes, I hope he comes.

Good. I think it is time that we have a chat about my relationship with James. Maybe I can meet up with Pete at the inn. Or, he can come over to James's place, where I have been living most of the time.

Great idea! I think it most definitely is time. Take care and say hi to James.

See you soon, honey!

Cassie released her shoulders and took a long, cleansing breath. She had to admit that she hardly ever mentioned James and Patsy in conversations with Pete, for fear that she might say too much. He really needed to be clued in to what was happening. What a great opportunity for a mother-son conversation.

Time for herself was rare these days, with all of the drama and happiness juxtaposed simultaneously, and swirling around Cassie. She decided to grab her journal and bike over to her neighborhood park, and pen her thoughts.

She vowed to do this more often, as a cathartic exercise and a focus on her feelings.

It was a chilly January day, and the sun was battling with the wind to prove their dominance as she raised her face and bathed in the splash of the sun.

On to February, the month of love.

Chapter Six - February

Cassie thought of Sundays as preparation days: lesson plans, laundry, meal planning, and grading papers. The more chores she did during the week, the less she had to do on Sunday. And, she worked around her Pete time, as that was sacrosanct.

One of the tasks that Cassie promised herself that she would fulfill this weekend was choosing some nutritious breakfasts that the Block Five 20 would create during the course of a week.

She found a breakfast sandwich with egg, cheese, and bacon or sausage on an English muffin or croissant. And there were two types of overnight oatmeal: cinnamon-raisin and strawberry cheesecake. There was the berry yogurt parfait and whole-grain waffle sandwich with eggs and bacon.

At their next meeting, Cassie distributed recipes to the class, along with a rating sheet.

"Okay, class. You will choose three recipes, make them, and rate them on a scale of 1-10, utilizing the following categories: simplicity, time, taste, and nutrition.

You will include the food groups in the nutrition category. You have one week to complete this assignment. Are there any questions?”

"Miss Greenwood! Are we allowed to ask our moms for help?" Declan asked.

Cassie thought that Declan probably hadn't put in many hours in the kitchen concocting recipes.

"Yes, you may, you little leprechaun. But the recipes, for the most part, should be created by you, so that you may fill out an accurate assessment."

Declan quickly raised an eyebrow, as if he was figuring out how to finagle his mother to do the cooking, solo.

The class went on to discuss a healthy intake of calories for a 15-year-old teenager: 2000 for a girl; 2400 for a boy.

Cassie showed a presentation with several types of food, and the class had to guess how many calories were in them. They were floored to learn that one of their favorite coffee drinks had 250 calories. And a hamburger packs a whopping 400 calories, the same as spaghetti and meatballs. French fries? Up to 400 calories.

"So, let's do the math. If you had a coffee drink for breakfast, fries and a burger for lunch, and spaghetti and meatballs for dinner, you would spend 1450 calories. But this is not including an actual breakfast item or snacks throughout the day."

Our Mother Away from Home

"For extra credit on the recipe assignment, please include the calories for your dishes." Cassie really wanted the class to gain more awareness about what goes into their mouths.

Heads bobbed up and down enthusiastically. The Block Five 20 willingly took up the recipe challenge.

Boy, I love these kids, thought Cassie. Even Declan, that little imp.

With only one week to go before the Sweetheart Dance, things were buzzing with the ASB kids. Voting for the king, queen and court—from the Junior Class only—was under way online. The juniors were the hosts for the dance, but all classes could attend. The court would be announced on Friday, so the students had a week to purchase dresses and rent tuxes.

Once again, the campus was resplendent in flowers, and, unlike Homecoming, Wendy from Wendy's Flowers and Gifts actually paid a visit, two of her employees in tow. Cassie was so glad that the dance was a week before Valentine's Day, taking some of the stress off. She confirmed with Wendy that she would be supplying flowers for the girls on the court.

In the midst of the craziness, she got a text from Pete:

Hey, guess what?

What?

No, guess!

You love me?

Other than that, Captain Obvious.

You are our DJ for the Sweetheart Dance?!!!

You got it! When you come up for air this week, I will treat you to dinner and we can have a little confab about the dance.

Sounds great!

Oh, yeah. I do love you!

Cassie just smiled. Back to chaos, she prompted herself.

Tina Caldwell popped in and assured Cassie that the March yearbook deadline was coming along nicely. And, yes, she had Albert Jones Photographers all set for the Sweetheart Dance.

"The next deadline will focus on winter sports, clubs, and the dance," said Tina. "We will also include the faculty and staff mug shots."

"Sounds good," replied Cassie.

That was a check off her to-do list.

She called James to confirm that this Saturday was the Marina Shores admin meeting, and, while she had a minute to herself, created her notes to share at the meeting. She left school at 5:00 and went home to run.

Our Mother Away from Home

On Saturday, Cassie and Pete drove to the Pelican Inn, and he brought her to Marina Shores after they dropped off their luggage. He was meeting his mother at the inn at 12:00 for lunch in the dining room.

Pete admitted to Cassie that he had mixed feelings about his mother's love life. Yes, she seems happy with her relationship with James, but, to the outside observer, it appears that she fell hard and fast for him in an instant. Poof! They meet and days later are completely wrapped up in each other's lives.

Patsy was nervous, but Pete needed to know the truth.

"Hi, Mom!" Pete greeted Patsy with a kiss on the cheek and led her into the beautiful dining room.

"Oh, Pete! This is gorgeous!" Patsy took in the vaulted, beamed ceilings, the central fireplace, and the comfy booths. "I can see why you like to accompany Cassie on her trips here."

After they chatted about their family—among other things, Parker's son, Drew would be having his 5th birthday in two weeks; Cooper, Patrick's son, made all-stars in soccer—Patsy addressed the 70-year-old elephant in the room. She had a feeling that Pete might want to avoid doing so.

"So, Pete, I wanted you to know that my relationship with James is going really well. As a matter of fact, I have been spending a lot of time at his home, which is about ten minutes from here."

"Tell me about him."

"Well, he is a widower. His wife died of breast cancer 10 years ago. He has 4 children and 12 grandchildren. Because he worked construction during summers, he knows a lot about the subject. He personally oversaw the remodeling of his home, which is huge. I guess it would have to be huge, to handle such a large family."

She concluded her mini-summary of James's life.

"This is his fourth go-round as a principal, and his last. He wanted to inaugurate a school one final time."

"Do you love him, Mom?"

"Yes, I love him very much. I never, ever would have thought that at my age I would find love again. As you know, I loved your dad with my whole heart, but I really missed having someone in my life all of these years. Now, I have that with James."

"Do you think that you will get married?"

Where was this coming from?   Pete shocked himself at the inquiry, especially since he'd been deliberately avoiding the subject of his mother's love life for months.

"Gosh, honey, I don't know. We really haven't broached that subject. We are just enjoying each other's company right now."

Pete nodded silently, as if he approved of the answer, for now.

Our Mother Away from Home

At Marina Shores, James called the meeting to order, and gave his report. All playing fields were completed, as was the Olympic-sized pool. Cassie's activities center was move-in ready (she grinned at that tidbit of information and couldn't wait for the keys), as were the front offices. And the math wing was completed, as was the campus store and adjoining student cafeteria. So, the campus was ready for the first students, and registration had begun.

Also, the advancement team was giving tours of the school, beginning in April.

Mike Stevenson noted all of the teams that were in the Ocean League, and shared that he and John Barrows, the Marina Shores athletic director, would be attending a district meeting with other athletic directors and vice principals in March. He also had a preliminary contract for Oakview Sporting Goods for team uniforms, sizes to be determined when the players were chosen.

All AP teachers were hired, according to a very pleased Claire Washington. Of course, all positions were tentative until the school had the numbers for those classes solidified. According to the district, AP classes had to have at least 20 students in each.

Last of all, Cassie, glancing at her notes, mentioned that in March there would be a mass email sent to all students who had registered thus far, asking for volunteers for ASB positions. Students had to submit an essay about their goals and fill out a questionnaire about any leadership positions in middle and/or high school.

She asked about the agenda item regarding the classes that could participate in certain dances, which was tabled last month. It was agreed that all classes would be allowed in the non-formal dances, and 10-12 classes for formal dances.

The group put on blue and green hard hats and embarked on a campus tour in security golf carts. It was chilly at the ocean, so Cassie was glad that she had a large windbreaker lined with fake fur given to her by the Bennington girls' water polo coach.

Using a speaker, tour guide James mentioned the points of interest along the way. His lively narration got everyone feeling excited for the coming year. Everything was pristine and inviting, like a postcard from the Chamber of Commerce.

From a public relations perspective, the school could sell itself. It is that top-notch.

Exhausted, Cassie dove onto the bed at the inn, and Pete joined her.

"Rough day?" he asked, beginning an impromptu massage, which elicited her immediate moans.

"Just a lot to take in for one day. But the campus is just beautiful. James gave us a guided tour. How was your lunch?"

"It was nice. My mom seems entirely in love."

"Oh, really?" Cassie feigned surprise. "That's wonderful! I want her to be happy."

"I know that I have been skeptical about this new romance of hers, but I am slowly coming around. We are all invited to James's house in a few weeks, to meet his children and grandchildren. That includes you, too, my pixie!"

"That's great! I would really love to meet them."

Cassie had heard James speak about his family many times, sharing stories about their escapades. She felt like she already knew them.

They spent the rest of the evening ordering room service and just enjoying their time together. No thoughts of tomorrow. No thoughts of school or KFUNN. Just the two of them.

On Monday morning, Ellie popped into Cassie's office with a surprise Iced Guava Passionfruit Drink.

"Oh, man! Thanks so much, Ellie! I could use this about now." Cassie's eyes lit up.

"I know you're under a lot of pressure. Just wanted to do a little to help out."

"That is so nice. And it's a real help. So, how is everything? You're okay to chaperone on Saturday?"

"Everything is great! Yes, I am chaperoning, and Sam is available if you need anyone. We can use some fun money."

"Absolutely, Ellie! Something came up with Libby Jackson, and she had to drop out. I was just sitting here wondering whom I could get to replace her. Can you run stuff by Sam? That would really help me."

"Great! This is his prep period, so I will swing by his room. I brought him a latte, so I will deliver that as well."

Good-hearted Ellie, Cassie thought. How I will miss her next year.

"Oh, and one more thing: The search committee chose Ronny Goldwyn as your replacement," said Ellie.

"Wow! Sam will be so happy!"

Wistfully, Cassie let it sink in: Her replacement has been chosen.

With all of the enthusiasm of day one back in September, the Block Five 20 chattered as they made their noisy entrance into Room 602. They were eager to share their gastronomical breakfast experience. Cassie knew why Porter was absent: Today is his meeting with the disciplinary board.

"So, I didn't like the oatmeal *at all*," announced Declan, loudly.

"Sorry to hear that, Declan. Let's see your numbers—take out your assessment chart. Tell me how you rated the oatmeal. What kind did you try?"

Declan was ready with the stats and came forward to the front of the class.

"Okay, I chose the strawberry cheesecake oatmeal. For simplicity, I gave it an 8. It was sort of simple to make, but you had to add a bunch of ingredients. For time, it is a 7. I had to take the time before bed to make it, and I missed out on playing video games for a while. Taste, a 5. I really don't like cheesecake, but I do like strawberries. As far as nutrition goes, I would say it was a 7. Yogurt is good for you."

He concluded, "The food groups were grains, fruit, and dairy."

"Good job, Declan. Did you do the extra credit?"

"Yes, I have the calories. With the yogurt, cheesecake without the crust, strawberries, granola, I have a total of 400 calories." Pleased with himself, he handed Cassie his paper.

"Sounds about right to me. Who wants to go next?"

January raised her hand.

"Okay, January, you're on. Come on up." Cassie liked to students to present in front of their peers, bolstering their public speaking skills.

"Miss Greenwood, I chose the breakfast sandwich on a croissant."

"Okay, let's have your ratings."

"For simplicity, I would say about a 7. This sandwich takes a while to make, if you don't already have the bacon or sausage cooked. Same with the time, a 7. As far as taste goes, I give it a 10. It was just delicious! For nutrition, I gave it a 9. I would have given a rating of 10, but croissants are really high in calories. You would save about 100 calories if you chose an English muffin. Food groups: dairy, grains, and meat."

"I would like to sum up with the extra credit. Calories, 600: 300 for the croissant, 100 for the egg, 100 for the bacon, and 100 for the cheese."

"Wonderful, January! You really did your research!"

Cassie could see that the Block Five 20 took a keen interest in nutrition, especially in the area of calories.

They had a test on nutrition next class, and the rest of the block went on to discuss drugs and alcohol.

It was late in the afternoon when Cassie texted Marco.

How are you? How was the meeting with the disciplinary board?

Pardon my French, but what a shitshow! Mom was crying constantly, Dad berated the kid over and over again, and the kid had to leave the room because he was nauseous. He ended up in the nurse's office. Everyone was looking for him.

Oh, man! Let's talk soon.

Cassie was taken aback. Pete had said that Frank Sheffield was such a nice guy, quote close quote. I guess you never know. Perhaps she can think of a game for the

class to play after their test, which might be a small comfort
for Porter.

The Sweetheart Dance gave Pete, Cassie, Sam, and
Ellie another chance to reconnect, even though they had
little chance to chat, between DJ duties and dance duties.

Nelson Party Planners did an excellent job with the
decorations for the dance at the Sheraton, with its theme
"Starry Night." There was a giant, dark blue sky above half
of the dance floor, with golden stars punctuating the canvas.
It reminded Cassie of the Vincent Van Gogh painting, which
she studied in an art history class in her undergrad years.

LED tea lights adorned the tables, along with white
bouquets and gold ribbons. The photo backdrop extended
the colors of the sky, and the whole effect was magnificent.

It was agreed that Cassie and Ellie would dress in
gold, and the guys would wear blue shirts. Before the dance,
they hit up the Albert Jones photographer and took couple
and group pictures. They even showed their silly side with
props, such as boas and oversized glasses.

"Starry Night" was a wonderful event for the
sophomores, juniors and seniors. The king and queen from
the Junior Class—Rosanna Truman and Curtis Mendoza--
were crowned mid-dance, and even the General seemed
pleased as she zipped around the ballroom, like one of those
robotic vacuum cleaners.

It was after midnight when Cassie and Pete said goodbye to Ellie and Sam and grabbed an elevator to their room.

They ate room service fare in the hot tub, with candles circling the tub, casting a romantic glow around the room.

An hour later, they were fast asleep on the very comfy bed. It was 11:00 the next morning before Cassie awoke and let out a little yelp, which doubled as a wake-up call for drowsy Pete.

"It's check-out time!"

"Relax, honey. I think they will grant us another hour or so to get our stuff together. After all, you're a really good customer."

"That I am!" She threw her arms around Pete, and gave him a loud smack of a kiss.

A quick call to the front office confirmed the extension, and they got to work packing.

The week was a busy one. On Wednesday, there was a combination letter of intent signing for senior athletes who committed to colleges and belated celebration for the championship football team.

A representative of the California Interscholastic Federation presented two plaques—for Bennington's state champions and for MVP of the game. Cassie was so pleased to see Zack Anderson get the MVP award and sign with Stanford, a Cardinal hat perched proudly on his head. Both his parents and Lexi's parents were present, she noted, missing Lexi.

When Porter Sheffield came back to class, he seemed more introverted and subdued than ever. Cassie figured that most of the student body must have known about the pot bust by now, as campus gossip is tantamount to wildfire. He is probably beyond embarrassed.

As a precursor to their discussion of drugs, Cassie set up stations around the room, asking for information, such as the definition of an opiate. She purposely omitted marijuana from the drug list.

The winners were Jenny Cooper and Sophia Bennington. Their prizes were pencils with congratulatory messages such as "great job!" and "way to go!" Porter kept to himself and had no desire to win this contest.

Toward the end of the block, Cassie had an announcement:

"Okay, class. Just a reminder that our blood drive is April 2nd. Even though it is two months away, we have some tasks to complete beforehand. One of them is to order shirts for the occasion.   Before you leave today, I want you to write your T-shirt size next to your name. You will be wearing your shirts the day of the blood drive."

The Block Five 20 scrambled to sign.

Their enthusiasm knows no bounds, thought Cassie.

After class, she ran by Ellie's desk, excited that the next day would be their little getaway.

"So, are you counting the hours?" Cassie asked her.

"Heck, yeah! I can't wait until we get the heck out of Dodge."

"Hey, off-topic, I wanted to ask you if you wanted to drop by Pam Roland's house with me next week. I need to solidify deets for the blood drive."

"Absolutely! I just have class on Wednesday night, as Monday is a holiday."

"Okay, I will contact Pam and let you know. Just wait until you see that nugget Preston. You will not want to put him down!"

Cassie confirmed with Pam that Thursday would be a good day. She asked about the T-shirts and got the information for the printing, which would actually be done by the Red Cross.

She had so much to do between now and April 2nd.

Before she left for the mini-vacay, Cassie needed to chat with Marco. She couldn't let that slide. She found him in his office, a rarity in the life of the head dean.

"Buttercup! How ya doing?"

"Just fine, Double L. Just wondering how everything played out with the board and the pot kids."

"The board decided to give the students three Saturday detentions, opting out of expulsion, because this was the boys' first offense. I notified the Boyds and the Sheffields, and outlined the dates with them."

"Thanks, Marco. I really worry about Porter. I think I need to refer him to personal counseling again, in light of recent developments."

"Good call, Buttercup."

Friday finally arrived! The couples took separate cars, as Pete had to return early on Monday morning for DJ duties.

They arrived at 6:00 at the West Temecula Winery, a beautiful venue with cottages instead of rooms and situated in an actual working vineyard. Guests were surrounded by grapes, which graced most of the grounds.   Amenities included the restaurants, tasting rooms, gift shop, and wedding chapel.

The evening was low-key, as the friends enjoyed wine by one of the many outside fireplaces and had a late dinner.

Pete offered a toast.

"Happy belated Valentine's Day!" The holiday was mid-week, and almost forgotten in the hectic schedule of four very busy people's lives. They enjoyed a late dinner before bidding each other goodnight.

More than a dozen hot-air balloons greeted the couples on Saturday morning, as they glided overhead and created a multi-colored tableau in the sky. People stopped to take in the glorious scene, reaching for their phones to document the moment.

The guys went for a run and the ladies opted for a massage, both great ways to begin the day. They would all meet up for breakfast in 90 minutes, recharged and ready for some adventures.

"I still am not sure about a balloon ride." Cassie felt her hands get clammy at the thought of being so high off the ground. She didn't even like sitting up high in the bleachers at a football game, and felt safer on the field.

"Well, we don't have to go up in one, or you can stay on the ground, and I'll go. Don't worry about it, babe."

Over bacon and eggs, the friends enjoyed the beautiful environment of the rustic restaurant.

"Look, everyone!" Ellie pointed out the window, where a bride and her side of the wedding party walked by, all smiles, glasses of champagne in hand. They had exited a party bus and, indeed, looked ready to party.

Five minutes later, the groom and his attendants exited their bus. A lively bunch, they preferred beer to champagne and were poised for a good time.

The couples spent the afternoon pool-side, then opted for a tour of the winery, culminating in wine tasting.

"I don't usually drink red wine, but I like this California red wine," Cassie said, holding her glass as if in a toast.

"What is the difference between Zinfandel and White Zinfandel?" asked Ellie of Graham, their tour guide. He was a dapper guy, with a bow tie, vest, and dress pants in the colors of the winery—red and gold.

"I am glad you asked." Graham loved to impart his knowledge of wine, as if he were a personal sommelier to each of his wine-tasting tourists.

"Zinfandel is made from a variety of black-skinned grapes. The grapes produce a robust red wine, which has as its primary flavors jam, blueberry, cherry, plum, and boysenberry. As you can see, we have paired it with white cheddar, turkey, and spiced apples."

Each featured wine included pairings of meat or pasta, cheese, and fruit.

"White Zinfandel is a semi-sweet rose', or blush wine. It is made from the same Zinfandel grapes as the red, but the difference is processing and fermentation. Before the fermentation process, the red grape skins are removed, leaving a hint of blush color. Pairings include pasta, gouda, and pears."

"I think we just ate lunch!" Cassie pointed out, rubbing her stomach twenty minutes later. "That was really yummy! Thank you, Graham."

Graham just glowed in response.

"Okay, what do you want to do now? We have all afternoon to play around until our dinner reservation at 7:00." Ellie queried the group, who pondered the possibilities.

"Well, just down the street is a casino," Pete pointed out. "Why don't we try our hand at poker or blackjack?"

"Wow, that sounds like fun!" Sam seconded the idea. "Why don't we all meet up out front at 12:00, and take one car?"

The casino was a noisy place with all kinds of sounds emanating from machines, and people. Pings, sirens, and bells bounced off the walls, inviting those at the entrance to join in on the fun. Winners let out whelps, jumped up and down, and high-fived their neighbors.

"Okay, what is your poison, Sam?" Pete was ready to challenge him, his competitive side emerging in the inquisition as he scanned the possibilities.

"I like poker. How about it?"

"Great! Ladies, we will be at the poker tables over in the center of the room. Come see us if you need anything." Pete took charge, and the guys headed over.

"So, Cassie. We have had a lot of adventures over these past four years, but we've never gambled together. What would you like to do?"

"Let's go to the slot machines. I am fond of penny poker, if they have it. I like to start small and work my way up."

Side by side, the ladies began a lively round of poker, where you could play any denomination from 10 cents to $3.00 for each hand. Cassie chose 10 cents. Ellie ramped it up to 20 cents.

This poker game was different; you could play 1-10 hands per game. Cassie was frugal, choosing 5 hands, and Ellie chose 10 hands.

An hour later, Cassie was up $3.00, and her BFF was up $100.00, having won a jackpot.

"Boy, that was fun!" Victoriously, Ellie cashed in her ticket, anxious to report on her winnings to Sam, who appeared serious as he contemplated his cards.

"The guys are still entranced with poker. Why don't we get a snack?" Cassie pointed out the food court, where there was an ice-cream parlor, among other grab-and-go restaurants. They opted for ice cream, but one scoop only.

"It seems like every time I go on vacation, I gain at least two pounds," Ellie said, slurping her cookies and cream.

"We have eaten well this weekend, but let's not count the calories. We can go back to doing that next week." Cassie was diving in to her butter brickle cup. "At least I ixnayed the cone!"

When they caught up with the guys, Pete looked miffed, and Sam looked self-satisfied.

"From what I recall," Pete said, glancing at his phone, "the term Renaissance man applied to guys in the years 1400-1600 in Italy. However, you are a damned 21st century Renaissance man!"

He continued, "You can teach biology, bowl like a champion, and play poker like you are a freaking professional!"

"Aw, you flatter me, Pete! Look at you, a famous DJ whose photos are on billboards and bus benches." Sam grabbed Ellie and put his arm around her.

"Hey, you should know this about our DJ," Cassie chimed in as she put her arm through Pete's. "He did a gig for Brittney Spears in Vegas."

"No, really?" Ellie was impressed.

"Yup, I spun the tunes for her for six weeks, during one of her residencies. She was really nice to me. That was right before my move back here from Arizona."

"And he tried out for the DJ job on *The Ellen DeGeneres Show*, but that went to that guy named Tricky," Cassie beamed at her man.

"tWitch, honey," Pete corrected, laughing. "He's a great DJ."

"Oh," he continued, "Forgot to tell you that Frank Sheffield is going to do a story on DJ PJ Panda. We are going to hit some golf balls next Saturday, and he is going to interview me that day."

He turned to Ellie and Sam. "Frank is a reporter for the *Oakview Register*, which is located in the same building as KFUNN. He is a devoted family man and a good writer, from what I have seen. We have become really great friends."

"That's nice," Cassie was a little circumspect when it came to Frank Sheffield, especially hearing about the disciplinary meeting from Marco. She was less than enthusiastic.

She let it drop, with a note to self: Contact Rachel Singleton for a check-in with Porter.

"Okay, why don't we go back to the hotel and hang out until we get ready for dinner? How about some pool time?" Ellie suggested. All agreed.

The West Temecula Winery pool was heavenly and huge. If you went underwater, you would hear music playing from speakers planted around the pool. Everywhere, one could see guests decked in hotel-issued red and gold robes. The whole scene spoke of relaxation of mind and body.

The ladies stocked up on books and magazines pre-trip, and delved into them as the guys played an impromptu game of volleyball with random people in the pool.

A waiter approached, and they ordered four mai tais.

What a great way to spend an afternoon, thought Cassie. Here with my favorite friend and our guys.

It turned out that Pete's team came out on top, so he recovered, somewhat, from his previous losses to Sam.

Dinner was served in the smaller dining room, with intimate tables dotting the room. Two fireplaces were blazing, casting a fiery glow in the candle-lit ambience.

"What do you want to do tomorrow?" Ellie was always the planner. She would make a great cruise director with her excellent organizational skills.

"Anything but the balloons," Cassie was still adamant about that activity.

"Well, I am up for a balloon ride, and Sam is, too," Ellie said. "What about you, Pete?"

"If Cassie doesn't mind, I would like to join you." Pete turned to Cassie, eyebrows raised in questioning.

"No problem, Pete. I can get a mani-pedi while you guys are in the air."

With that, it was settled.

The couples returned to their cottages, and Ellie agreed to book the balloon ride for 9:00. Cassie went online and made her appointment for the same time.

Sunday made its arrival with crisp, clear skies—perfect for a hot-air balloon ride. Pete, Ellie, and Sam hopped into their basket, with the help of their guide Sebastian. They joined the colorful cavalcade, and waved to Cassie as she headed to her appointment. She was a bit late, but couldn't pass up the chance at seeing her peeps in the air.

The mani-pedi provided the ultimate gift of relaxation. It assuaged Cassie's fear of ballooning and gave her a chance for some me time. As a matter of fact, she fell asleep during the foot massage, one of the best massages she'd ever had.

The couples regrouped for lunch in the outdoor café. Though it was February, it was unseasonably warm, those blue skies beckoning them outdoors.

"Oh, Cassie! It was wonderful!" Ellie was effusive about the balloon ride over lunch.

"People on the ground looked like ants that far above. The countryside was so gorgeous, it took my breath away. Everywhere that the eye could see were trees and rolling hills of green. It was a beautiful experience."

The guys echoed Ellie's sentiment, and all agreed that this would be a first, but not a last.

Cassie and Pete left Sunday evening, as he had an early call at KFUNN on Presidents' Day.

On Monday afternoon, with some precious time on her hands, Cassie decided to stop by the Pizza Project, as she hadn't seen Bruno in weeks. As soon as she entered the restaurant, the aroma of garlic and oregano gloriously attacked her senses, but something else stopped her in her tracks. It was Bruno, behind the counter, eyes red-rimmed and stature deflated.

"Oh, Cassie!" He came around for a hug, especially needing one about now.

"It's my Maria! She has breast cancer, and needs a mastectomy as soon as possible. What will I do if something happens to her?"

Cassie caught the eye of Dori, one of the college students who works for Bruno, and mimicked a drink with her hand, and nodded towards a row of booths. She led Bruno into one, all the while with her arm around him.

"I am so sorry, Bruno. Tell me about it."

She listened to Bruno describe his "one and only" and her diagnosis. He began to cry; this huge man, so caught up in emotion, seemingly appeared to be shrinking with each tear.

Cassie learned that Maria would have surgery at the end of the week, and she promised that she would be in touch.

Dori brought over glasses of water, and Bruno took a Bruno-sized drink.

"Okay, give me your phone, Bruno. I need to give you my contact information, and I will get yours, too. Please promise me that you will call me if and when you need me."

"You are so good to me, *cara*. Thank you."

Later, when he was off his shift, Pete called Cassie, and she filled him in on poor Maria. He knew just the song that he would devote to her the next day.

"Hey, KFUNN Nation! This song goes out to the wife of a special friend, who is going through a rough patch right now. I send my special thoughts to both of you during this challenging time."

With that, he played "My Maria," by B. W. Stevenson, a fitting tribute to a strong, brave lady from her beloved.

Glad that she was able to catch the dedication, Cassie just smiled. Good one, Pete.

Our Mother Away from Home

The next weekend, Cassie volunteered to supervise a playoff boys' basketball game on Friday night at Bennington. The gym was packed, with blue and silver casting a radiant hue among the bleachers on the Bennington side. Some Jets infiltrated the sparsely-populated Simcox Sentinels' side, as the school was two hours away, and not many chose to make the trip.

Bennington won, 66-64 and would play in the state finals the next week.

Saturday, Pete spent time with Frank Sheffield, hitting balls at Oakview Municipal Golf Course and hitting the beer and pizza at the Pizza Project. In Pete's mind, the visit to the Project was two-fold: friendly conversation/lunch with Frank and watchful observance in Bruno's absence. Of course, he was prompted to dine here by Cassie, who was at the hospital visiting Maria a day before her surgery.

Pete and Frank developed a quick, easy friendship. Pete was glad to have a new friend, as many of his high school friends had married and moved away from the area.

By sheer coincidence, the two of them both graduated from the University of Arizona, with Frank at the Walter Cronkite School of Journalism and Mass Communication, and Pete majoring in arts and media. Go Wildcats!

Frank told Pete that he adored his wife Gloria and his son Porter. The three were planning a vacation to San Diego during spring break, which would include trips to Sea World and the Wild Animal Park.

On Sunday, the meeting of the Castleberry and Patterson families finally commenced. It was preempted by

T-ball games, DJ gigs, a baby shower, and an emergency with the plumbing system at Marina Shores High School.

Pete, Patrick, Parker, and their significant others met James's children Lauren, Julia, Tom, and Bobby, and their husbands and wives.

Altogether, there were 16 adults and 16 children for Sunday lunch, skillfully orchestrated by Patsy, the ultimate party planner.

It was as if James were prescient in his design of the house, which was perfect to accommodate this huge crowd. An extra-large island with a sink provided the centerpiece of the kitchen. There were two ovens and two dishwashers. The last piece of new construction was a sunroom off the dining area, which seated 30 people. Add a few kiddie tables, and everyone had a place to sit.

It turned out that Patrick's son Cooper is in the same kindergarten class as Bobby's son Trevor. When the boys saw each other in front of James's house, they ran toward one another and hugged like kindergarteners would— robustly, lovingly, and without reservation.

Bobby's wife Claudia is an aide in the pre-school at their school, Oakview Elementary.

The meeting turned into an impromptu celebration—of family, of love, of food, of good cheer. After clean-up, the games appeared—Scrabble, Clue, Monopoly. Corn hole, basketball, and a full-sized swing set were options for the outside crowd, working off the feast as the chilly late-February ocean breeze provided a misty hug.

When Cooper took a hard fall off a swing, Patsy rushed to bandage him and dry his tears. There was a measure of comfort having a nurse among this group who always traveled with a black bag, similar to a doctor's satchel.

When things calmed down, she sat with James on the love seat—with one toddler in her lap and two in James's lap. She took in the scene, close to tears of joy at the happy chaos surrounding her.

Indeed, this was the magical month of love. Abundant love.

Chapter Seven - March

"Oh, Cassie!" Bruno exclaimed excitedly through the phone, his voice booming with equal parts relief and devotion. "*Il miracolo*! It is a miracle! An absolute miracle!"

Maria had, miraculously, pulled through her mastectomy with no complications. The surgeons were confident that they got all of the cancer. Her re-construction would be ongoing for the next month, and it was agreed that their son Mario would manage Pizza Project #2. He already knew the restaurant inside and out, having worked there during high school and when he attended Walker College as a business major. At 29, he was a bachelor with a vision. It was an unspoken expectation that Bruno and Maria would one day hand the baton off to Mario, as general manager of both restaurants.

"Bruno, I am so glad!" Cassie had been holding her breath for days, praying that Maria would triumph over the cancer. All of the important aspects of her days seemed diminished in anticipation of a good word from the hospital.

"I will come and visit Maria when she returns home," Cassie promised. "Please let me know if you need anything at all."

On Thursday, Cassie and Ellie paid a visit to Pam Roland after school. In the past few months, Preston had changed tremendously, sporting two lower teeth and crawling all over the house, which didn't seem as pristine as Cassie's last visit.

More baby accoutrements were added: a swing, a walker, more toys, and a bouncer that hung from a door frame.

And Pam looked a bit on the exhausted side.

"Oh, guys! It is so great to see you!" She hugged her friends as best she could with a chubbier Preston at her hip. "Tell me everything that is going on!"

"Pam, this little guy is growing so fast!" Cassie reached for him when Pam handed him over. "These little arms and legs have what I love most about babies—fat rolls!"

Preston smelled heavenly, all powdery and fresh. Must have just been changed.

Ellie couldn't wait to do the same.

After the baby-go-round, Cassie and Pam got down to business.

"We have sent the shirt sizes to the Red Cross, and I have been in touch with them about volunteers," said Cassie. "Our nurse, Sandy Klein, has arranged to have a substitute nurse in for the day. I have also gotten volunteers from Oakview General."

She continued, "Online sign-ups are in progress, and my class is doing a commercial tomorrow after we get the big blood drop costume sent over from a Red Cross volunteer. I already have a student willing to wear the costume and another one who will cover the commentary. Jet TV will also be on hand for filming."

"Gosh, Cassie! I think you have covered all of the bases. Oh, one more thing: You will need to purchase some orange juice and crackers for the students to have post-draw. Save your receipt for those items, and present it to Ms. Daniels after the drive for a refund. I have my sister coming to babysit that day, so I can provide moral support. I can help with your students and the call slips for volunteers. Make sure you contact the front office with their names."

"Pam, that is fabulous! I feel so much better having visited you. And Preston is an adorable baby bonus! Tell me, how is it all going?"

Pam filled them in on daily life at home, but there was a wistful expression on her pretty face. Her emotions posed a conflicting juxtaposition: She missed the adult contact and conversation, but treasured her time with Preston, precious but challenging.

Our Mother Away from Home

Perhaps she will look into some mommy and me groups in her community that might fulfill both desires.

A few hours later, Pete texted.

How's my pixie doing today?

Oh, Pete! We visited Pam Roland and little Preston this afternoon. Ellie fell in love with that little nugget. That's what I like to call him. He is just this little chunk of a baby, with fat rolls and two teeth.

Did you get everything squared away for the blood drive?

Yes, thanks to Pam.

Hey, I had a wild idea. Why don't I join you that day? I can broadcast my show outside of the gym while the volunteers are coming in, to help pump them up. I can bring some stuffed pandas to randomly give away. I haven't brought them over to Children's Hospital in a long time.

Pete! You are brilliant! I think it is a great idea! And your mom will be here!!! Why don't I run it by the administration tomorrow at our meeting? I hope Constance gets on board.

All right. Tell her I won't be so loud as to disturb the classes. But, as I recall, the gym is a bit removed from the classroom buildings.

Thanks so much! Love you!

Love you, too!

At the administrative board meeting, Constance reported that intent to return forms will be sent to all faculty and staff in the next week via email. The forms are a declaration to return for the next school year, to not return, or to have a return predicated on something.

Cassie always found it interesting when the administration received these forms. One art teacher wrote, "I will return if I don't have Patrick Gregory in my class next year." A biology teacher requested that "I will come back if you fix the faculty women's bathroom in the 800 wing. It is disgusting!"

Of course, it is sad when some opt to leave for various reasons.

Constance also mentioned that one of the track coaches is under investigation by the district. Word on the street is that he has been having an inappropriate relationship with a senior girl. Of course, everything is confidential between administrators.

After everyone had shared their reports, Cassie broached the subject of bringing in Pete for the blood drive.

"One of the DJs from KFUNN, Pete Patterson, has volunteered to broadcast from Bennington on the day of the blood drive. He would be situated at the front of the gym, and get the kids in a good mood before they give blood. He promises not to play the music loudly, as to disrupt the classes."

"Cassandra, I am not sure about this." Of course, Debbie Downer—aka Constance—would put the kibosh to the idea.

Tom chimed in.

and Freshman Class Officers would be chosen the next weekend.

She went to Marina Shores on Friday, having taken a personal day, and completed the interviews on Saturday, when all offices were complete. Pete wasn't with her, so she decided to go home late on Saturday afternoon.

On Monday, Cassie decided to check in on Lexi Cassidy and Zack Anderson.

Zack came in during his aide block.

"Tell me, Zack. How are you?" Cassie cut to the chase.

"Great, Miss Greenwood. I feel bad, though. And a bit guilty.   I am all psyched about going to Stanford, and Lexi is a little depressed about putting the baby up for adoption."

"Has she sought counseling?"

"Yes, she has been seeing Dr. Singleton. Oh, and we are in constant communication with the gay couple who are going to adopt him. Oh, did I tell you that it is a boy?"

"Wow! Wonder if he will be a football player like his father?"

"I sure hope so!"

Cassie felt wistful in her exchange with Zack. Who knew what the future would bring for the little man?

After Zack left, she phoned Lexi. Her previous communication had been via email, but she felt the need for closer contact.

Lexi was happy to hear from Cassie, but she did sound depressed, as if her exuberance was strained.

"How are you feeling?"

"Oh, I am coming along. Been gaining weight, and wondering how I will fit back into my cheer outfit after the baby is born."

"That will come in time, Lexi. Just worry about your health and the health of your baby in the time being."

She continued, "I know that you were experiencing a bit of depression the last time we were in touch. And you have been seeing Dr. Singleton. How is it going?"

"I feel comfortable with her. But I have something important to ask you, and I was hoping that my mom and I could meet you for frozen yogurt sometime?"

"Absolutely! When are you free?"

"How about this afternoon?"

"Okay! Meet you at La Crema at 5:00?"

"Sounds great!"

Lexi looked so huge, but so adorable in her maternity dress. Like any mother two months away from giving birth, she held her bump with both hands, as if in protective mode. Or, more like it, proud mama mode.

Mrs. Cassidy was as warm as ever, hugging Cassie and touching Lexi's stomach.

While they were eating their pre-dinner treat, Lexi broached the subject that she was anxious to put on the table.

"Miss Greenwood, would you please come to the hospital when I give birth? I know that I won't have a lot of time with the baby, but I do want you to meet him. You have been such a strong support for me and Zack."

Cassie instantly teared up, touched at the request.

"Absolutely! Thank you for asking, honey. I do not share my contact information with students, but I will give it to your mom. She can let me know when you have gone into labor."

"Thank you, Miss Greenwood! I really appreciate it, and I know that Zack will, too."

After hugs all around, Cassie went home to spend some time with her journal. So much was happening so fast, she had to catch up on life itself.

On the weekend, she, Pete, Ellie and Sam were invited to Bruno's house for Sunday dinner, an event in itself.

Our Mother Away from Home

His entire family joined in the feast, which came in waves. The appetizer was spaghetti, the entrée lasagna, and the dessert tiramisu.

And it was so great to see Maria, looking frail but happy, with one of her 10 grandchildren planted on her lap, serenely sucking on a bottle.

The prognosis was good for her, but she was unaccustomed to taking it easy. They had been managing the restaurants for over 30 years, so she was used to always being busy.

Bruno was bustling around, but he stopped to see to her needs, his main focus of the day. His miracle had survived.

Just like James's house, Bruno's was designed for a crowd. He was enveloped in all of the love surrounding him, and he treated his friends as family too.

Mario, the restaurants' heir apparent, stepped in to help everyone feel welcomed.

Pete was even enlisted to spin some tunes—with actual vinyl records. Chief among them was "That's Amore," which brought an impromptu family sing-along. Everyone knew the lyrics, and swayed back and forth in unison.

When he thought no one was looking, Bruno bent down to steal a kiss from his wife, who lit up and seemed to glow, despite her fragile condition.

This is what I want, thought Cassie. Messy, chaotic, rowdy family life. Love times forever.

And, if I ever get married, I want Bruno to walk me down the aisle.

Chapter Eight - April

April 1st. The Block Five 20 was excited for the blood drive tomorrow, as Cassie distributed their T-shirts. She was shocked that the boys just peeled off the ones they were wearing, and replaced them with the shirts that bore one of the standard Red Cross slogans: Heroes come in all types and sizes. It was one of the slogans that January used in the commercial.

Cassie had hand-delivered shirts to Patsy and Pam, her ulterior motive for the latter being a chance to visit her favorite nugget.

Instead of replacing his shirt, Porter asked to use the restroom, and returned with the new shirt on. Was it modesty, or just the need to use the facilities?

Note to self: Chat with Bart Childress, coach of the Boys' Sophomore Baseball team. She wondered if he stripped in front of the team.

The next day, the clamorous scene at Bennington resembled more a rally than a blood drive.

Our Mother Away from Home

Or maybe a circus.

As promised, Pete had a little visit with the General, which proved to be an interesting conversation.

"Ms. Daniels, it is nice to meet you," Pete shook her hand upon entrance to her office. He felt Ellie's eyes bore through his back.

"Thank you for coming in, Peter. I just wanted to ask about the procedure today."

Pete, taken aback to be called by his formal name, described how he would be playing music at the gym entrance as kids came in to give blood. He had lots of stuffed pandas to give away randomly throughout the day and gift cards to local fast-food restaurants.

"I understand that you are dating Cassandra."

The General just had to punctuate their conversation with that comment, which seemed an accusation rather than a statement of fact.

"Yes, we have been dating since September."

"Well, so be it. Just make sure that the music is not too loud. And I would appreciate a lack of PDA in front of the students." Thus ended lecture number 610.

As if! Suddenly, Pete felt such strong empathy with Cassie, and he couldn't wait to join her after school for a post-drive early dinner.

Declan, in his element, assumed the role of host for the day. He high-fived volunteers, Pete, and the Red Cross people. Wherever he went, he seemed to bounce.

He and January did their BLOOD cheer about ten times and composed a THANKS cheer.

Cassie had the cafeteria staff set up a burger bar for lunch for all volunteers. The kids enjoyed choosing all of the toppings for burgers and fries. A favorite among the students: chili cheese fries.

"Mom!" Pete was so excited to see his mother as she showed up for her afternoon shift. They exchanged hugs and caught up.

"How is James doing?"

"Oh, he is so busy at Marina Shores. But things are really coming along, so much so that we are stealing away to Maui during spring break! I cannot believe we are making this happen."

"That's great, Mom! Cassie's inside, if you want to get situated."

"Thanks, dear."

Pam Roland was instrumental in the flow of the day. Her focus was on the Block Five 20, as she orchestrated call slips and kept in constant contact with all of them. Her replacement, Neil Williams, volunteered to help during his free block. It gave them a chance to chat curriculum. The two spent time with nurse Sandy Klein, who was on hand for support and blood draws. There was a substitute nurse from the district who took her place for the day.

When the final bell rang, Declan looked exhausted as he extricated himself from the blood drop costume, yanking it off like the celebrity contestants on *The Masked Singer*. The only thing that was missing was a chorus of "Take it off! Take it off!"

The Red Cross volunteers stayed until 4:00, in the event that any parents wanted to give blood after school. Cassie joined the parents in last-minute blood draws, though she admitted that she almost fell asleep on the table. She also learned that her blood type was AB negative, not a common type according to Sandy.

Though she didn't have much time to visit with Patsy, just her presence was a comfort to Cassie, as she had become something of a second mother to her.

Altogether, 100 pints of blood were collected, an amazing feat with a school of 350 students. Constance was very pleased and would express her thanks on Monday during announcements.

Cassie and Pete crashed at her house, but had enough energy for a two-person bubble bath.

"I am so grateful for your help," Cassie said as she rubbed bubbles all over Pete's back, and began to massage his weary muscles.

"Oh, Cassie, that feels so good. I don't know why I am so beat. I think it's being around teenagers that saps energy out of a person."

"I am just used to having the station manager and maybe another DJ around me. Except, of course, if I am on location. How do you do it?"

"Believe it or not, being in the midst of teenagers makes me feel younger. I have the opposite reaction—they seem to energize me. Except for today!"

Somehow, they found the strength to walk to Cassie's bed and tangle in the covers. They were passionate in their lovemaking, which had evolved to another level of need. As they lay in the aftermath, they were interrupted by the doorbell. Talk about lousy timing.

"Chinese food! Crap, I forgot that I called for it! An hour seemed like a long time when they gave me the ETA. That sure went by fast!"

Pete got up quickly, found his pants, bolted for the door, and over tipped the driver.

He filled Cassie in on his talk with his mother.

"Hey, my mom told me today that she and James are going to Maui over spring break. Isn't that great?"

"Well, I knew that James has turned Marina Shores into a well-oiled machine, so I am not surprised. Good for them!"

"I had an interesting chat with your principal today. What do I call her? Constance? The General? Ms. Daniels?

Anyway, she asked me if we were dating. It was so weird. I almost thought that she was going to ask about my intentions toward you."

"Oh, Pete! I am sorry that she put you through the ringer! I envisioned her asking about the volume of the music."

"Oh, I got that, too. I am glad that things worked out so well today. Maybe we can do some more networking at the school sometime."

Cassie kissed Pete, silently expressing her thanks and her hopes for another collaboration.

The catching up continued. "Forgot to tell you that Frank Sheffield finally did the profile on yours truly. Let me get it in my car."

At the mention of Frank, Cassie remembered her promise to herself, to visit Porter's coach. She also had a physical reaction—the hair on the back of her neck stood up, as it did with red flag situations. And any mention of Frank.

"Okay, here is an early copy of the people section for tomorrow's edition. My story is on page two."

Cassie read aloud:

On the first floor between the Oakview Tribune *newsroom and the office of Jeremy Meyer, DDS, in the Commonwealth Building is the home of KFUNN radio, number 105.7 on your FM dial. Every morning from 6 to10, DJ PJ Panda spins the tunes for the morning drive commuters. Offering only the best hits from the '70s, '80s*

'90s and today, KFUNN is a popular radio station, and DJ PJ Panda—aka Pete Patterson--is equally popular.

Not bad, Cassie thought, as she read on about Pete and his listeners, who all gushed about him.

"Too bad the article was already finished, or Frank could have sent over a photographer to Bennington today, to see you in action." Cassie would have liked that.

"I think he was running a bit late on it, so he had to finish up. He seems really preoccupied lately. As a matter of fact, he stood me up for lunch yesterday at Primavera. Gina felt so bad for me that I got a huge helping of spaghetti.   I hope that everything is okay with Frank."

Cassie was so glad that tomorrow she would not be making her way to the ocean because she was exhausted. In fact, her schedule was clear for the weekend. She liked having serendipity on her agenda: *Que sera, sera*. What will be, will be. That sounded so nice about now.

The next week, Cassie spotted Bart Childress mowing the infield grass.

"Hi Bart! How are things looking for the season?"

"We're off to a good start! We already beat Oakview and Glendale, so 2 in 0."

"Great! Hey, I wanted to talk to you about one of your players, Porter Sheffield. What's he like around the other players? This may seem like a strange question, but do boys at the sophomore level shower after practice?"

"Not a strange question. We have practice after school, and the boys have the option of showering, or just going straight home. Porter opts for the latter."

He added, "He has a fine pitching arm, and he might be moved up to junior varsity towards the end of the season."

Cassie, ever curious, had to probe.

"What do you know about his parents?"

"Dad is one aggressive dude. Kind of hard on the kid—but needlessly so, as he is a wonderful athlete. Porter cowers when Dad gets loud or criticizes him, like he just wants to hide. He is embarrassed and hurt simultaneously. I worry about him. I have even referred him to the personal counselor."

"Oh, Bart! I have, too! Okay, I promise you this: I will get to the bottom of the situation, so that you and I both have peace of mind."

"Sounds good, Cassie. Thank you so much."

That afternoon, Ellie and Cassie had a girls-only happy hour at the Pizza Project. Time seemed to keep slipping away from the two BFFs, who needed to re-connect.

"Spring break is in two weeks," Ellie announced. "Sam is going on a destination bachelor party weekend with his brother, the groom, and they have plans to travel the rest of the week, just the two of them. Kind of a last-minute trip before Brad ties the knot. So I am free!"

"Great! I know that Pete has to work that week, so I am free, too!"

"Okay, let's plan."

Arranging the perfect chick getaway, they decided to return to the West Temecula Winery, and made arrangements for three nights in a bungalow.

"I have got a brilliant idea!" Ellie was bursting at the announcement. "Why don't we invite Pam? I think a girls' vacay would do wonders for her. And it's perfect timing because Mitch is off that week. Even if she can only stay one or two nights, it will re-charge her batteries."

"What a great idea! I will call her when I get home, and give her the details." Cassie never underestimated Ellie's insights. She would be a great psychologist.

Bruno popped in as they were leaving, and they enjoyed their hugs and catching up with him too.

"Ladies, thank you so much for your support for my Maria. The reconstruction is finished, and she is just taking it easy. Mario has already taken over at the Pizza Project #2, and things are going well there."

He added, "I really enjoyed having you over for dinner. How are your young men doing?"

After updates, the phone rang and the ladies left, but not before spotting Mayor Max and Harley crossing the street to PP, hand-in-hand. They looked so good together, and their cheerful and positive personalities matched.

"Max! Harley! So great to see you guys!" Ellie greeted them. "How have you been?"

"Well, we just got engaged!" The guys held up their left hands simultaneously, sporting rings that resembled wedding bands. It was a double-beaming.

"Wow!" It was Cassie's turn to effervesce. "When are you getting married?"

Max explained, "We are getting married in October in the town square. Everyone in Oakview is invited, and it will be potluck-style. Constance is going to be the officiant."

Cassie had no idea that Constance was licensed to perform weddings. Well, well. Again, the woman remained a total mystery.

When the Block Five 20 regrouped after the blood drive, everyone had a lot to say. Their pride in the accomplishments of the day shone on their faces as they chattered about the volunteers, the music, and their job as call-slip runners.

"That blood drop costume was hot," complained Declan.

"Oh, you little leprechaun! That is why I scheduled your breaks with Mrs. Roland."

"I know, but *still*." Always a comment, thought Cassie, who was eager to thank all of her students personally.

"Everyone, I want you to know how proud I am of you and all of your hard work on the blood drive. Altogether, the Red Cross collected 100 pints of blood, which is quite amazing for a school our size."

"Declan and January, your cheers were a highlight of the day! Thank you for making the extra effort to create and perform them. As I said before, you are a wonderful team."

"Thanks, Miss Greenwood." Declan half-blushed. "Hey, I talked to your boyfriend all day. He seems like a really nice guy."

"That's very nice of you to say, Declan. Yes, he is a very nice man." End of story.

The class switched gears and started the chapter on first aid.

"Okay, class, let's take a look at the matching worksheet on how to treat different injuries with the help of first aid. This is a pre-test to see how much you know about first aid. Please swap papers with your neighbor.

"Let's see what your answers are. First off, what do we do for burns?" Cassie made a note to self to get someone from the fire department to demonstrate first aid. Anything for a hands-on experience with this group.

They continued to break down the first aid procedures, giving examples. In a departure from the norm, Porter came forth with a question.

"Miss Greenwood, does ice really help with bruises? I, ah, sometimes get hit by a baseball and have different colors as the bruise gets better. I don't know if the ice really helps."

"Well, Porter, the book says that the ice can reduce the size of the bruise, which may allow it to heal faster. The cold temperature from an ice pack makes the blood in that area flow more slowly. It may reduce the amount of blood that leaks out of your vessels."

"Thanks."

"You might mention this to the other players, in case they get bruises, as well. Any other questions, class?"

January asked about fractures, which occur often with cheerleaders.

"Fractures are to remain stable, so that means that you need something like a board to attach to the leg, for example."

"Okay, now that we're finished grading, please tally up the scores."

The next weekend at Marina Shores would be the sole gathering for April, as spring break beckoned for everyone.

Cassie didn't understand the concept of spring break! Sometimes it is the week before Easter, sometimes the week after. Sometimes it was permanently set on the first week of April. It all depended on the district, she imagined.

James gave a run-down on all buildings, which are now complete. All sports fields were finished, as was the pool. City building inspectors were slated to converge on the campus that week to give their final approval on the buildings and evacuation plan.

Cassie shared that all ASB and class officers were in place. ASB camp would be held in the mountains of Big Bear during the second week of June, giving everyone a chance to meet and to interact before the school year began. She would send out an email to the teachers and staff already hired to request volunteers for class moderators, who would serve as chaperones.

At the camp, the students would decide on the school's first theme of the year, and themes for all of the dances.

Cassie planned a scavenger hunt at camp, which would double as a getting-to-know-Marina-Shores game.

"Everyone, thank you for your input," James concluded. "Have a wonderful spring break."

He pulled Cassie aside after the others had left.

"Patsy and I were going to ask you and Pete to take us to the airport on Monday after Pete's shift, if that is okay."

"Sure, James! We would be glad to."

Monday at noon, Cassie and Pete drove the Maui-bound couple to the Oakview Municipal Airport. All around them at the luggage check-in, boisterous people in Hawaiian attire and leis seemed to float off the ground, steeped in happy anticipation.

Our Mother Away from Home

"You guys have fun!" Pete said. "We will see you on Saturday. Aloha!"

The couples hugged goodbye, and Cassie felt wistful, thinking that Maui would be the perfect honeymoon destination.

She spent the night with Pete before leaving for Temecula and her vacation with Ellie and Pam. She held him close for a long time before sleeping. He was the rock of her life, and she could depend on him for always being there, despite the craziness that was happening in her life.

Even though she was staying just two nights, Pam found the little vacation a shot in the arm. Forty-eight hours of baby-less play time, surrounded by two ladies bound for a fun adventure.

The group arrived late the first day, then spent the next day poolside, before moving on to the casino. After dinner, it was karaoke time at their hotel.

"I think that Helen Reddy is rolling over in her grave about now," announced Cassie as they returned to their bungalow. "'I am Woman' is an anthem for womanhood, not a soundtrack to drunken karaoke!"

The ladies all burst into uproarious laughter, flopping onto the beds.

"Hey, that guy was really into you," Cassie reminded Ellie about the karaoke emcee who kept staring at her and offered to buy her a drink three times. He had movie-star good looks, a masterful physique, and was dressed to kill.

"Totally not interested! I've got my guy at home, waiting for me!" declared Ellie. Ever the event planner, she made a suggestion: "I have an idea. Let's pretend that we're the Golden Girls and order some cheesecake from room service."

Within 30 minutes, they were having a midnight snack of the decadent dessert, planning for tomorrow, Pam's last day before leaving in the afternoon.

Moving a bit slowly, the ladies entered the dining room for breakfast the next day. They headed to the pool afterward and relaxed the whole day, their worries and responsibilities temporarily shelved for now. They swapped magazines and stories. Pam left in the late afternoon.

"Ladies, I had so much fun! Thank you for including me on this little getaway."

Poolside, Pam had confessed that she and Mitch were trying for another child, and this trip could prove the calm before the happy storm of being a mother of two. She also recently joined a mommy and me group, which met in the park at the center of her housing development every Wednesday morning. It was a great network of young moms, who were sympatico with one another and shared concerns about such subjects as daycare and pediatricians.

She hugged the others and practically skipped out of the bungalow, thrilled to have experienced this escapade.

Our Mother Away from Home

On Saturday, Pete and Cassie headed to the airport to fetch his mother and James.

As the invigorated travelers descended the escalator into baggage claim, Cassie saw that they had matching shirts which proclaimed "Just Maui'd."

Oh, she thought, they just came from Maui. That's the meaning of the shirts. How cute. Then she instinctively glanced at Patsy's left hand and was temporarily blinded by the bling.

Just married!

"Hey, you guys! How was the trip? How was Maui?" Pete just went on and on, oblivious to the message on their shirts.

"Honey, look at this," said Patsy, pointing to the shirts. "It means that we were just married in Maui!"

She held up her left hand to blind him, as well.

"Oh, wow!" Pete, stupefied, could utter no more words than the two. The whole concept of his mother having a new love life had him mystified, but he had no idea that things were this serious.

James came forward, addressing Pete.

"We know that this is a shock, and we are going to have a reception soon. But we thought that Maui would be the perfect backdrop for our nuptials. It was so beautiful, and we were caught up in the spirit of the island. I hope that you will be happy for us."

"Yes, of course." Pete shook his hand, then hugged his mother. Cassie hugged them both.

It would take Pete some time to adjust to the fact that he has a stepfather and stepsisters and stepbrothers.

He envisioned holidays in the future, chaotic but fun, and, surprisingly, he smiled at the thought.

Welcome to our blended family, James.

At Bennington the next day, Cassie was just going to fill Ellie in on what had transpired the previous day when she got a group text from Sandy Klein, sent to her, Marco, Constance, Christine, and Tom.

"Please come to the trainer's office ASAP. Please. Emergency!"

Cassie burst through the door not four minutes later, only to be bombarded by a frightened and trembling Porter Sheffield.

"Miss Greenwood! Please!"

With that, he wrapped his arms around Cassie and never wanted to let go.

Chapter Nine - May

"To quote Marco, 'What a shitshow.'"

Cassie was slumped over in her office chair, facing an equally exhausted Ellie in an adjacent chair. It had been a grueling, gut-wrenching past few hours.

Since Porter's impenetrable grasp, the administration had discovered, via Sandy Klein, that little Porter's body was riddled with bruises in a place that one wouldn't normally observe—his torso. It was a typical place for an abuser's blows, and, in this case, a child physical abuser.

Sandy was administering check-ups for the spring sports teams when she placed the stethoscope on Porter's back. He winced in pain. Slowly, she lifted the back of his shirt and gasped. Porter froze.

Constance became a very effective whirling dervish, contacting chief of police Bryan Stanley, Mayor Max (for his legal expertise in family law), and Child Protective Services. She immediately put out an all-points bulletin for her administration to get to her office, pronto.

She got a temporary restraining order against Frank Sheffield, who could not be within 200 yards of Bennington. With Bryan's assistance, Frank's wife Gloria did the same. She had called a few family members for support, as she appeared to be very fragile, on the verge of hysterics. Max ended up taking her and Porter home, as Gloria was in no condition to drive.

On a tip from one of his friends, Frank was found at the Rusty Anchor bar, face-down in a vodka tonic, minus the tonic. He was immediately taken into custody by one of Bryan's men.

Turns out that Frank had become addicted to narcotics, after suffering chronic back pain from a car accident a year earlier. One of the side effects of abusing narcotics was the development of harmful behaviors. Frank had decided to take out his depression and pain on Porter, his human punching bag. His 95-pound punching bag.

Cassie had thought to mention going to the Pizza Project, but she, quite frankly, had no energy to even make mention of it, let alone get out of her chair and move.

Pete arrived at about 7:00 to come and get her; and Sam, who had been working in his classroom during the hubbub, as advised by Ellie, emerged as well.

When he and Cassie were alone, Pete looked into her eyes.

"I am so sorry that I misjudged Sheffield and questioned your feelings for him," he said. "I know that, as an administrator, you couldn't share information, even with me."

Our Mother Away from Home

He continued, "I could see your reaction every time Frank's name came up. There was this look on your face that I rarely see. Perhaps it was a look of disgust. I should have been more attentive to your feelings. Crap! I had no idea that this person who at first seemed to have it all together would morph into such a monster. I feel so sorry for his wife and son."

He gathered Cassie up in his arms, and she couldn't stifle the tears that began to flow, releasing hours of tension, emotion, and pain.

Those arms had become a new refuge for her, a place of safety that she had never known before. All that she wanted to do was to stay with him and to forget the events of the day.

"Take me home," she said, a plaintive look on her tear-stained face.

Amazingly, the student body was not clued in to the drama that transpired in the trainer's room, thanks to the discretion of Sandy and the administration.

Porter was absent the next day and wouldn't return until the following week. He and his mother had gone to live with her sister.

Baseball season was coming to a close, and Cassie thought that Porter was probably torn about the effects of his absence on the Boys' Sophomore Baseball team. She would pay a visit to Bart to explain the situation.

Our Mother Away from Home

While Cassie was trying to emotionally recover from what she and Ellie would subsequently call The Incident, Zack Peterson knocked on her office door.

"Hey, Zack. What's up?"

"Well, I have all of the dates for the opening of the Stanford football season, and our practice schedule. My parents will be coming up for family weekend in September, and we have a home game against UCLA while they will be there."

He seemed excited at the prospect of his parents seeing him play college ball.

"That's great! You can give them a tour of the campus, if they don't get one on move-in day. Tell me, how is Lexi doing?"

"She is like a cute little beach ball! She is anxious to return to school and to the cheer squad, but she knows how important it is to be healthy for the baby, so she is taking it really easy."

"That's good. I will give her a call this week. I don't know if you know this, but she asked me to drop by and see the baby when he is born. I gave her mom my contact information."

"We will appreciate that, Miss Greenwood. You have been so supportive to both of us, and we are so grateful."

"You and Lexi are wonderful people, and I am so glad that I have gotten to know each of you in a different way, beyond your status as students at Bennington."

Our Mother Away from Home

When Zack got up to leave, he turned to Cassie and touched his hand to his heart.

He quietly whispered "thank you" before turning for the door, wiping away tears that suddenly appeared.

Two weeks later, Cassie got a call from Mrs. Cassidy. Lexi was in labor and being rushed to Oakview General Hospital.

It was 10:00 in the morning, and Cassie flew to Ellie's desk, explaining in as few words as possible that she needed to fly out of school. Luckily, she didn't have the Block Five 20 today.

At Oakview General, she parked in the structure and rushed to the maternity ward.

There, she caught sight of Zack, his parents, Lexi's parents, and, inexplicably, Mayor Max and Harley.

She did a double-take.

Then, it dawned on her: They were the gay adoptive parents. Oh, wow. Cassie would process that tidbit later. Now, she had to focus on the impending birth.

She hugged everyone, and hugged Max extra tight. She had so much respect for him, and she was happy that he would get to add "parent" to his life's roles.

An hour later, Zack emerged from the delivery room with a tiny bundle in blue and placed him in Max's arms.

Our Mother Away from Home

It was a beautiful thing to behold, a treasured moment that Cassie wouldn't ever forget. The room was awash in emotion, and she was so glad that she was witness to this little miracle.

That little baby meant so much to everyone present. It was equal parts loss and a relinquishment for the Peterson and Cassidy families, and an amazing new chapter for the soon-to-be-married Max and Harley. She spent a moment to absorb it all, and, after her parents visited with Lexi, she spent some time with her.

Lexi was in tears, but they were happy tears at successfully giving birth to a 7-pound, 9-ounce baby boy, one that she and Zack had come to call Matthew Allen.

Cassie silently prayed that, one day, Lexi would be blessed with more children.

With an eye toward the end of school in six short weeks, Bennington was ablaze with posters for candidates running for ASB and class offices.

Declan capitalized on his success at the blood drive, and threw his hat into the ring for Junior Class President. His posters read "Declan, he's your man! Vote McIntosh for President."

The Bennington twins were the only two sophomores running for treasurer of their class. Sophia's posters said "Vote Sophia for Junior Class Treasurer. It just makes cents!" Her brother's posters proclaimed "Make your Mark for Bennington for Treasurer!"

Each candidate was allowed one 30-second spot on Jet TV, which ran extra-long Monday through Thursday, with the voting on Friday. All posters had to be removed by 4:00 that day.

Cassie was glad that the voting was online. It made the process so much easier than physically counting ballots. She brought in all of the candidates Friday afternoon and announced the winners.

Declan won by a mile and did a little impromptu happy dance all around the activities center at the news.

Cassie had no choice but to give the twins the title of co-treasurers. The voting was that close.

Exhausted, she left school close to 6:00, came home, and flopped on her bed, fully clothed.

So much was happening and she took to her journal to chronicle it. She barely thought of the upcoming Prom, and was glad that the drama with Frank Sheffield was in the rear view mirror.

At least, she thought it was, until the next week.

Constance had stayed late after school that Friday and didn't get to the parking lot until 9:00. She had gone to dinner with Tom Reynolds, and went back inside to answer some emails after Tom left.

Rain was beginning to fall softly as she made her way to the faculty parking lot. No security guards were present, a red flag that prompted her to make a mental note to contact Tom, whose job includes management of the security staff. Perhaps the guard assigned to the parking lots was making his or her rounds.

She threw her purse, raincoat, and umbrella into the back seat, and rushed to take the driver's seat. Unknown to her, Frank Sheffield occupied the passenger seat.

Constance let out a scream at the sight of him. He looked disheveled and smelled of liquor. With about three days' worth of beard and his hair matted and unwashed, he resembled a homeless person in grave need of a shower.

"Drive, bitch!" He yelled at Constance, placing his 45 caliber gun at her neck, making a circular impression in her skin.

"Mr. Sheffield! You are disobeying court rules about staying away from Bennington. Did you not understand the stipulations of the restraining order?"

"Screw that, bitch! All I know is that you took my family away from me, and you have to pay for that!"

"Mr. Sheffield, you must know that it was your actions that took your family away, not the actions of the administration. We had to follow protocol for the sake of the safety of your wife and son. Please, I beg you. Put that gun down!"

His booze-addled brain was moving helter-skelter as he pressed the gun even further into Constance's neck. He had no real plans for a destination. It was the journey that he sought, and he considered ending that journey with a bullet straight into the principal's brain.

Our Mother Away from Home

Constance's tears were in contention with the rain, as it came pelting down now. Her characteristically stoic demeanor gave way to utter fear and confusion. Her heart was racing, and her hands were glued to the steering wheel, frozen in place.

Sheffield must have posted bail somehow, she thought.

"Where are we going?" Constance pleaded, afraid to take her eyes off the road, concentrating to see clearly.

"Just drive, bitch! Drive!"

Constance drove the hilly pathway away from Bennington, amid the prolific oak trees that lent the town its name.

Sheffield started to shake uncontrollably, perhaps a druggy aftereffect, perhaps the effects of a lack of drugs. Sweat poured down his face and dripped onto his now-sodden shirt.

The pistol was still trained on Constance's neck, but he kept losing focus and, at one point, clumsily dropped it between the two seats.

"Keep driving!" he yelled as he scrambled to retrieve the gun, which he fumbled and accidentally fired. The bullet ricocheted off the console between the seats and lodged itself into his chest, heart-adjacent.

Sheffield cried out in instantaneous, grueling pain, grabbing his chest and flailing side to side.

Our Mother Away from Home

Constance was aghast and again tried to concentrate on the road ahead of her, when a deer darted in front of her path. As she veered the car to the side, she crashed into a tree, heaving forward as the airbag deployed.

Sheffield was thrown against the windshield, which cracked upon contact with his glass-bathed head. He hadn't been wearing a seatbelt.

The next thing that Constance remembered was the sound of sirens as she was whisked into an ambulance in the pounding rain, unaware that Frank Sheffield had died, ultimately, from the bullet wound and not the windshield impact.

Days became a blur as she had two surgeries to repair internal and external damage that the accident had caused. Oakview General had a blood supply on hand for her type, but more might be needed for subsequent surgeries. The Red Cross had been contacted for a possible match and would search their records of recent blood drives.

In discussion among the Bennington administration, and, by orders of the school district, it was decided that Cassie would be interim principal in Constance's absence. The next few weeks would be incredibly busy, with Prom on the horizon and the end of school just four weeks away.

Porter Sheffield returned to school looking surprisingly upbeat. Maybe at the source was relief that his father would no longer be abusing him. He put all of his energy into his studies, and, perhaps more importantly at the moment, the end of the baseball season.

Cassie was glad that she spoke with Coach Childress, who stepped in and kept close tabs on his player, who exhibited even more promise than at the beginning of the season.

Porter didn't know it yet, but Bart intended to move him up to varsity if the team went to the playoffs.

The Marina Shores administration was having its weekend meeting mid-May, but Cassie requested that she miss it, as pressing matters at Bennington needed addressing. James was very understanding, and said that he would fill her in later.

Pete seemed to be at peace with his mother's marriage and vowed to get to know James even better. The two had even planned a fishing trip next month, when Pete began a two-week summer vacation.

And Pete was at peace about the realization that his good friend turned into a demon, capable of abusing his own child in the frenzy of drug dependency. He knew that, if blessed with his own children, he would treat them as his greatest treasures, and hold them close always.

One sunny Saturday afternoon, he and Cassie decided to go for a bike ride in Covington Canyon, the site of their hike in the early days of their relationship.

The weather was on the cusp of becoming hot, but was perfect nonetheless. In a few weeks, pools would be occupied, and shorts and flip flops would make their appearance.

They stopped at a park in the canyon, and Cassie retrieved picnic items from her bike basket. Under the shade of a grand oak tree, they feasted on sandwiches and fruit.

"You know what, my little pixie?" asked Pete as he emerged from the comfortable silence that they had been accustomed to. "Even though things have been crazy lately, I am so glad that you have been by my side through it all. You say that I am your rock, but you are mine. I love you."

With that, he gave her a peanut-butter kiss and held her for a long time, just taking in her sweet scent, which he would be content to do forever.

A few days after Constance's second surgery, the Red Cross contacted Cassie and asked her to meet their representative at Oakview General Hospital the next day. Cassie was perplexed, but agreed to the visit, even getting a substitute for the Block Five 20.

Constance was still not allowed visitors, so Cassie wouldn't be able to drop in for a chat. But that was okay with Cassie, who didn't want to bombard the patient with questions. She, Tom, Christine, and Marco were muddling through without her guidance, but it would be nice to run some things by her.

In a meeting room at Oakview General, Cassie was introduced to Elisabeth Lathrop of the Red Cross. Elisabeth was all business, clipboard in hand, cutting to the chase.

"Miss Greenwood, as you know, Constance Daniels is here at Oakview General, having had two surgeries already. She could possibly have a third. "

She continued, "Because her blood type is rare, we are searching for donors with the same type, and asking them to donate blood in her name. We understand from your school nurse, Sandy Klein, that you have the same blood type as Constance, AB negative. Would you consider giving blood?"

"Absolutely. Just let me know where to go."

The next day, Cassie dropped by the Red Cross center on her way to work. She still was in awe of the fact that she and Constance had the same blood type, but that thought flew by the wayside when she set foot on the school grounds. So many things to accomplish in so little time, she thought, reflecting on the imminent end of the school year.

As she was making notes in her planner, Tina Caldwell knocked on her door. She handed a piece of paper over to Cassie. It was her letter of resignation; she was giving three weeks' notice, and her departure would occur after finals.

"I just wanted you to know that I am leaving Bennington and taking over Jonathan Bennett's sales territory for Harvard Yearbooks. Jonathan is moving up to regional manager."

"But what about the Bennington yearbooks? When will they be arriving?"

"They should be here right after Memorial Day. I will be around to deal with any snafus before I leave."

Cassie now had to hire a new yearbook adviser ASAP. The staff would be attending yearbook camp in July, so an adviser needed to be in place well before then. Maybe Sam, with his endless creativity, would be interested in the job.

Note to self: Contact Sam.

"Thanks for letting me know, Tina. Hey, I wanted to ask you about your second job as a hand model. Have we seen you in magazines or commercials?"

"Yes, I am the model for Skin Soft lotion, in both commercials and magazines. And look for me in the next Coldplay music video. My whole body is in that one."

With that, she left Cassie's office, her nose leading the way.

Prom was held at the Oakview Sheraton, and the theme was "All Aboard." The backdrop in the photo booth was a cruise ship and props included leis, sunglasses, and captain's hats.

The king of the Prom was January Propst's brother Alex, a senior baseball player who committed to the University of San Diego. Turned out that January actually went to the dance with Declan. Were they a couple? Hard to say. But their undeniable chemistry was begun with their blood drive collaboration. It seemed to escalate from there.

Pete gladly took to the tune-spinning at the Prom, and many of the students who knew him from dances and his time spent at Bennington came by to visit with him. He felt like a local celebrity, as if he should be signing autographs. He did have lots of requests for selfies, which he gladly honored. Good PR for the station, he thought.

Before the dance, the Pizza Project supplied appetizers for pre-dance munching. Bruno, Maria, and Mario Bertolli were on hand with finger foods such as meatballs on toothpicks. Much easier to handle than spaghetti or lasagna, especially with formal attire.

When clean-up was done, Mario approached Cassie.

"He's a lucky guy." He nodded his head in Pete's direction.

"Aw, thanks, Mario."

"I thought about asking you out, but it would be like asking my sister out."

Cassie laughed so hard that some students whipped their heads around in her direction.

After the requisite "Bennie and the Jets" ended the evening, Cassie strolled over to thank Pete.

"Again, you were fantastic!" she said. "Want to come up to my place upstairs when we are done?"

"Absolutely! Let's have a midnight snack."

The students filed out a bit past 11:00, and the chaperones canvassed restrooms and hidden spaces for stragglers.

Marco checked in with Cassie.

"Hey, Buttercup!

"Marco! I haven't seen you in a while. Everything okay?"

"Well, during the crowning, my team did our usual sweep of the limos. One of them had water bottles filled with vodka. We spent the past half hour waiting for the parents of the Boozy Ten to come and get them. The kids were all stunned to be pulled from the festivities prematurely."

He continued, "I guess the vodka was for a post-dance celebration because they all passed the Breathalyzer test."

Cassie just groaned in reply, thanked Marco for his diligence, and bade him good night. He would take care of all of the details and, as always, she had total faith in him, and trusted him implicitly.

She turned to Pete. It was time to close the books on the dance, to snuggle into the arms of her one and only, and to forget the high drama that May ushered in.

Chapter Ten - June

"Just think of it as a McIntosh apple! It is something to remember me by."

Declan plopped his gift onto Cassie's desk, a ceramic red apple with a smiling worm coming out of it. Of course, there would be a worm! Seemed a fitting metaphor for the gifter.

"Thank you, Declan! I will cherish it forever."

"Hey, is it true that you are our principal now?"

"Yes, it's true. Ms. Daniels is healing from an automobile accident, so I have stepped in to be the principal until the end of the year."

"Cool. Really cool." With that, he gave her a thumb's up and smiled.

The Block Five 20 was ready for their final exams, filing in with sharpened pencils in their hands and smiles on their faces as they took their seats for the last time in Room 602.

Our Mother Away from Home

Looking especially happy was Porter, who was elevated to the varsity level for the team's playoff games. Tomorrow would be the first round, and he was slated to pitch. He looked as if he had been gaining weight, which was a great thing, considering how scrawny he was when he began his sophomore year. Cassie heard through Max that Porter's mother Gloria was doing better, and both she and Porter were returning to their home in Oakview.

When the final was over, Cassie told Ellie that she was going to visit Constance at Oakview General. Constance was cleared for visitors, so this would be a perfect time to stop by.

Cassie was scanning the hospital for any sign of Patsy when she was approached by the visitors' center attendant.

"May I help you?"

"Yes, I would like the room number of Constance Daniels, please."

"Okay, please give me your name for this sticker, and proceed to room 2-505."

Constance appeared diminished by her surroundings, swallowed up in a large bed that seemed inconsistent with the usual hospital-issued beds, her arm attached to an IV.

Cassie just sat and waited for Constance to wake up. She, herself, dozed off in her chair.

"Oh, Cassandra! How nice to see you!"

Cassie woke up to the greeting. She had to concentrate to remember where she was.

"Constance, how are you? You gave us a really good scare at Bennington."

"I am doing better, thank you. I am glad that Frank Sheffield is not here to torture his son any longer."

"We all are."

"Cassandra, I don't know if you were asked to give blood for me, but I appreciate it if you did."

"I sure did. I thought it strange that you and I have the same blood type."

"Well, yes. But it is not *that* strange. Sit here." She patted the bed, summoning Cassie.

"I need to tell you something very important. All I ask is that you just listen."

Constance's voice was weak, but she summoned the courage to say what she had to say.

"I have kept tabs on you all of your last 32 years. Whether it was winning the spelling bee in eighth grade to your softball awards, I have been aware of your successes. And your tragedies.   I have newspaper clippings of your games, and I even attended some of them. I was at both Bennington and Cal State Monterey Bay and witnessed your graduation from both."

Cassie was speechless. She just sat in silence, which beckoned Constance to continue.

"Even though I lived far away, I subscribed to the *Oakview Register,* both in print and online, on the off chance that you might be in the newspaper. And I made several trips to California over the years."

"At one of your Bennington games, I met Patsy Patterson, now Patsy Castleberry. She was waiting in the bleachers for her son's game, which was after yours. We struck up a conversation, and we have been in touch since then. I couldn't believe it when she started dating James, whom I have known since I moved here. I am so happy that they found each other."

"Oh, Constance! Why are you telling me all of this now?"

"I am telling you now because it looks like I may need one more surgery. Every time I go in for an operation, I fear that I may not survive...and I just had to let you know that I am your biological mother."

Stupefied, Cassie just listened, mouth agape.

She finally spoke. "Why have you been so hard on me, if I am, indeed, your daughter?"

"I am so sorry for being harsh. I didn't want to play favorites. I treated you like I treated everyone else at Bennington, and I shouldn't have. Please forgive me."

She continued, "I figured that you had no desire to contact me, or you already would have, and I just wanted to be near you. When I found out that your parents died, and that the principal job was open at Bennington, I snapped up the opportunity to come and be near you. I am just so glad that the district chose me."

Our Mother Away from Home

Just then, a nurse entered the room to dispense medication. Constance asked for just a few more minutes alone with Cassie.

"You must be wondering where your father is. He is an English professor at the University of Notre Dame. We are still in touch. I have shared news about you over the years. If you want to meet him, I will give you his contact information."

"Did you come from Indiana, then?"

"No, I lived in Chicago before I came to Bennington. I was principal at a huge high school in the suburbs. It had 3,000 students. I was glad to leave there and come to Bennington, especially to be in your presence."

Cassie couldn't speak. Her father, an English professor. Wow. Just wow. And Constance, the General, her mother.   She couldn't immediately wrap her head around it all.

So many questions swirled in Cassie's mind. What happened between Constance and her father? What was her father's name? Why did they break up? Is he married to someone else, and does he have a family?

In time, she would gain answers to these questions and more. But she needed to focus on the present, to get to know Constance in a different light. Beginning today.

Epilogue

Under a brilliant blue October sky, Max Dunlap and Harley Keffer were pronounced husband and husband, with Constance officiating at the gazebo in the town square. In Max's arms was little Elliott James Keffer-Dunlap, a flaxen-haired, five-month-old baby. He was named after his parents' fathers, Elliott Keffer and James Dunlap. He would be known as EJ.

It seemed that all of Oakview was present to witness the nuptials. Tables were laden with potluck dishes that the mayor's constituents brought to the celebration.

Constance had graduated from a wheelchair to a walker to a cane. Her surgeries were successful, and she decided that this was the right time to retire, as she had slowed down considerably since the accident.

Ellie was sporting a one-carat diamond engagement ring, as happy as ever with Sam by her side. Her fiancé had been named High School Science Teacher of the Year in June, and was invited to teach a three-week summer course on innovative lesson planning to brand-new teachers at Walker College. As for Ellie, she kept her feet firmly planted on Bennington soil, choosing to stay when Cassie was named the permanent principal. She wouldn't become a private investigator or a romance novelist, and that was just fine by her.

Lexi was present at the wedding this glorious fall day with her fellow cheerleaders, all in their blue and silver uniforms. After the wedding, the Jets would be playing a day football game against Oakview. Lexi seamlessly slid back into Bennington life and was looking forward to sending her application to Stanford, where Zack was flourishing. She even went with the Petersons to family weekend and was so proud to see Zack playing football.

With college scouts already scoping him out, Porter moved up to the varsity level after his team won the state championship at the end of last year. He seemed to be thriving in his junior year and even started dating Sophia Bennington. Cassie had found out that his mother Gloria had found a job counseling abused women. It was discovered that she, too, had been abused by Frank.

James was extremely gracious when Cassie had to let go of the Marina Shores job to become Bennington's principal. As it turns out, Katie Francis, who had applied to become the activities director at Bennington, also applied for the Marina Shores job, and got it. There was a sigh of relief from Cassie that it all turned out.

Patsy brought her copious party-planning skills to Marina Shores and became Katie's assistant. Patsy's focus was on dances, and she was perfect for the job, organizing themes and planning decorations with Nelson Party Planners.

Our Mother Away from Home

Cassie had moved out of her office and into the principal's office so that Ronny Goldwyn would occupy hers. So far, he had done a great job as Activities Director.

Of course, the wall of love moved with her.

In her office now, she scanned all of the photos and reflected on the past 33 years of her life.

What a full life it had been, punctuated by tragedy and triumph, loss and renewal. She had found the man of her dreams, her rock-solid protector through all of the changes and challenges she encountered.

In time recently spent with Constance, she learned that her father's name was David Cummings, and his specialty was Shakespearean studies. Apparently, Cassie came by that naturally. Constance also told her that she and David were together in graduate school at Notre Dame where they met, and the decision to give Cassie up for adoption was mutual when they discovered that Constance was pregnant. They split up soon afterward.

No doubt about it: Cassie absolutely wanted to meet her father.

But for now, she had a mother to get to know and a job that demanded her complete attention.

And, in two weeks, she was in for a huge surprise that only Declan and Pete knew about.

Declan would be the emcee of the Homecoming Rally, as it is the job of the Junior Class this year. After Mayor Max crowned the queen, Declan would call Pete to the center of the gym where Cassie stood.

On one knee, and with the entire school watching, Pete would propose to Cassie, who stood with her hand over her heart and tears staining her cheeks.

And Declan would be beaming, his face and fist thrust skyward in salute to his mother away from home.

About the Author

After having taught high school English and journalism for many years, Tanya Katnic traded in her teacher's podium for a writer's desk in crafting this first novel. With her twin sons married and on their own, she lives with her husband and a very overprotective basenji dog in Southern California. Years ago, she gained inspiration for the title of this novel when a student asked her: "Aren't you supposed to be our mother away from home?"